DRIVING IN THE DARK

DRIVING IN THE DARK

Deborah Moggach

Thorndike Press
Waterville, Maine USA

This Large Print edition is published by Thorndike Press, USA.

Published in 2002 in the U.S. by arrangement with T.C. Wallace, Ltd.

U.S. Softcover   ISBN 0–7862–4257–4 (General Series Edition)

The text of this Large Print edition is unabridged.
Other aspects of the book may vary from the original edition.

Set in 16 pt. New Times Roman.

Printed in Great Britain on acid-free paper.

Library of Congress Cataloging-in-Publication Data

Moggach, Deborah.
     Driving in the dark / Deborah Moggach.
        p.   cm.
     ISBN 0–7862–4257–4 (lg. print : sc : alk. paper)
     1. Bus drivers—Fiction. 2. Fathers and sons—Fiction.
    3. Separated people—Fiction. 4. Large type books. I. Title.
     PR6063.O44 D75 2002
     823'.914—dc21   2002022888

CHAPTER ONE

If only women had four wheels. They'd be easier to understand, wouldn't they?

I'm thinking about one day in September, when I came home and found all my belongings in the front garden. It was starting to drizzle; there were my records, and my woodworking tools and all my back copies of *Motor Sport*, getting damp.

I thought at first that my wife was having a clean-out. To tell the truth, I was surprised. She wasn't fond of housework. Besides, it puzzled me that none of her stuff was there, filling up the lawn.

I didn't have a clue. I'd been away on the Isle of Man, on a Weekend Break, and my back was playing up. I went into the kitchen and there sat Eleni, smoking. The ashtray was full, which was a bad sign. She was usually well-groomed but she had a ladder in her tights, probably from carting all my stuff out.

She said: 'My brother's coming round.'

'Pardon?'

'My brother's coming round with his van. He'll help you with your things.' She repeated, patiently: 'Costas, my brother.'

I thought: why does she have to explain who her brother is? I know him. She had put on too much of that blusher stuff; it made her look

1

like an actress.

Then she said: 'I can't be having you here any more.'

That was an odd way of speaking. For a moment I thought she was referring to one of her usual annoyances—my rotary lathe, something that tripped her up. But then I realized that she was referring to me. She sat there, tapping her white cowboy boot and looking at me as if she had never seen me before. It was then that I realized what she was saying.

She already looked different. Her face looked as if it had been a little bit reassembled, like somebody's face does when you've just learnt their name. Her cheeks were two pink smears. She stared at me as if I shouldn't be standing in my own kitchen. I thought of the six coats of Ronseal I'd put on the units.

'Did you hear me, Desmond?'

She never called me that. I heard the rain pattering on the veranda and I thought of my *Motor Sports* and knew I shouldn't be thinking about them. I felt a surge of anger, that she had never exerted herself like this before, on my behalf. It must have taken her ages to fill up the front garden.

She said: 'I don't want to be married to you any more.'

I replied: 'But we haven't started yet.'

I don't know why I said that. She got up and

2

went into the lounge. I heard the ting of the phone; she was probably ringing up her family.

I meant that we had been married for six years and there were so many things we hadn't got round to yet. I had hardly told her anything about when I was little; there hadn't been time. On the other hand, she had never asked. On the other hand, too, I didn't know nearly enough about her. Sitting in the coach that morning, waiting for my passengers to embark, I had listened to *Only the lonely*. The name Roy Orbison had never been mentioned by either of us. That name; lots of others. Lots of things. Suddenly I felt as if all the bones had been taken out of my body. I sat down.

It's a funny thing about time. I didn't know how long I sat there. It was like being in another country and all the clocks were wrong. I heard her, a mile off, still talking on the phone and even the kitchen seemed to have changed shape. It wasn't the room I had known; the walls were further away. I felt dizzy, and thought it might be a good idea if I went upstairs to sleep. I would pull the duvet over my head and when I woke up the front garden would be back to normal and she would be in the bathroom, having a bath. She liked spending ages in there; I had made it really luxurious.

I nearly moved, to go upstairs. Then I remembered her complaints about my sleeping. 'He's such a lump,' she would say to her girlfriends, nudging me in the ribs. 'Snoring in front of the telly.' I had presumed that this was said in the normal, exasperated way that wives talked, but now I would have to remember everything all over again.

Stupid things popped into my head, like how was I going to pick up my dry cleaning when she had the tickets? I needed to know the answers but I didn't dare ask her in case she started explaining and then it would be real. I stood up to get a can of lager, but then I sat down again. I had no breath in my chest. The phone tinged; she had finished speaking.

I didn't want her to come in because then she would tell me when she had stopped loving me. Perhaps she would tell me that she had never loved me at all. I wanted a cigarette but my jacket was in the hall, and I would have to pass the lounge door. I stayed dead still, like an animal scenting danger. I felt I was suffocating in a sitting position.

Then I heard the front door and Costas, her brother, was in the hall. He had let himself in without ringing the bell. This was alarming; it must be a crisis. Costas stood in the hallway, looking bulky and embarrassed. Both rooms were too dangerous. He caught my eye, shrugged and spread out his hands. *Women*, he meant. I nodded. I had always liked Costas. In fact, I liked Eleni's family more than she did, but now she had called them and they would have to close ranks. Her sister Maria had

4

arrived too. Suddenly I was outnumbered by Greeks.

Costas came into the kitchen.

'What's got into her?' I asked. My voice surprised me, it was squeaky.

'Search me.'

We were silent for a moment, listening to the female voices in the lounge. Women had so much to talk about.

'Seems a funny thing to do,' I said.

'You know Eleni.'

I wasn't so sure about that. I said: 'Sorry you had to come all the way out here, in the rush hour.' We lived in Orpington, in the suburbs. He lived in London.

'It's Sunday, mate.'

I had forgotten what day of the week it was. I twitched back my cuff, furtively, to look at my watch. It was 9.20, way past the rush hour. I hoped I wasn't going mad.

'You know anything about this?' I asked.

Costas shook his head. 'Only this morning.'

Then he rummaged in his pocket, took out his cigarette packet, took two out and lit them. He passed one to me, and it was such a simple thing to do that I burst into tears.

*   *   *

And that was the end of my marriage. It all happened so quickly. Overnight my life changed, as if I had been arrested for a crime I

5

hadn't known I'd committed. It had a momentum of its own, so fast it took away my breath. Overnight something happened to my house in Croxley Road, it was like Eleni's face changing, and when I went back I was a visitor. Eleni wore a new blue sweater and it hurt my feelings, not just that she had had the spirits to shop—and to spend my money—but that in it she looked separate. It suited her, too—it was a fluffy thing that clung to her waist—and I realized: *One*: that I'd be buggered if I complimented her now, and *Two*: that I hadn't complimented her enough in the past.

That, she told me, with Maria in attendance, was one of my many shortcomings.

'Remember when I had my highlights?' she told Maria. 'He didn't notice it for a whole evening and then he said there was something funny about me.'

'I'd just had three days at the Blackpool Illuminations,' I said.

'What's that supposed to mean?'

She rolled her eyes at Maria and lit another cigarette. Chain-smoking was the only sign that she was going through a hard time. I had come back for the last of my stuff and I'd had to make my own Nescafé. She must have felt it was easier, not to be friendly.

'He was never interested in my dancing,' she turned to Maria. 'Remember when I got on Yorkshire TV? Did he turn up to watch?'

'I was on that Tulip Tour,' I said. 'I had

thirty-three senior citizens to look after. I was in blinking Holland.' I didn't add that they had cut that bit anyway. When the programme had come on I'd driven her all the way to Bradford, to the only mate I knew who lived in the receiving area. It was a children's TV story about a ballerina, and we had all sat waiting in this chap's living room, he'd even invited the neighbours, and we'd waited for the dance routine bit to come on and it never had. The drive home had been awful.

'Honestly, he drove me round the bend,' she said. 'Sometimes I felt like screaming. I used to go into the bathroom for a good bellow.'

So that was what she did in there. It always smelt of bubble bath but I was probably insensitive. There had been no point to any of it—the grouting, the varnishing, the time I had held her head all night when she had been eating mussels. I felt terrifically sleepy—more tired than I had ever been in my life. But I couldn't just lay down on the settee; it wasn't my home any more. She would tell me how boring I was—correction, she would tell Maria, who had already heard how I slept through TV, and snored in bed, and had once actually fallen asleep while . . . well, it was only the once and nobody should have heard that, not even a sister. I'd had glandular fever and I'd been plastering the lounge all day, and couldn't even a husband be human, once in a while? I'd apologized enough at the time.

7

They started talking in Greek. She said something like *aglocas* and *pracoras*, but I couldn't understand. Maria replied with a stream of *k's* and *l's*; they were more vivacious in their own language.

It grew darker. Maria listened, shaking her head in sympathy. This irked me. For six years Eleni had complained about her sister, saying how bossy and disapproving she was. Now, overnight, they had become chums. Maria had temporarily moved in. They were waiting for me to leave, so they could make their supper and talk about me more.

'He was always halfway up a bloody ladder with his Black and Decker,' Eleni said, coughing through the smoke.

I was going to reply that I was making a home for her, that I loved doing it and thought she loved it too, but I didn't. It made me too sad.

*   *   *

I drove back to London. I know I was a wimp, letting myself be pushed out of the house like that. But if I got angry she might phone a lawyer, she was so hysterical, and then it would all be official and have to happen. If I laid low it might blow over. After all, she had been hysterical before, though in the early days I had called it fiery and admired her for it. Once she had bought a new dress, and when she had asked my opinion I had said it was quite nice. I hadn't been concentrating. So first she hit me and then she took the dress into the garden and burnt it. It was made of some nylon stuff because it shrivelled and smelt strange.

I hadn't known what to do with her. Men seemed simpler than women. Sometimes—I could admit it now—sometimes it was a relief, going to work in the morning. It was like coming into the fresh air. There they were in the depot, horsing around. 'Wotcha,' they'd say, and I'd say 'wotcha' back.

How did other blokes manage it? There were seven of us working for Reg, and most of them were married. But they all had children, one way or another; that seemed to settle things back home. Mind you, Reg had four kids, lovely children, and that didn't stop him carrying on with Sonia in the office. He'd kept Sonia going for years and nobody had thrown his belongings into the front garden. It didn't seem fair.

I said nothing at work. This was partly pride. Years before, Eleni had come to the depot. She had been wearing her red PVC coat and white boots and they'd all whistled at her. She was ten years younger than me and ever so pretty—slim, skinny actually, with big eyes and sheeny olive skin. She looked fragile and yet bold; she walked as if she expected to be whistled at, which was half the trick. The rest of her family was running to fat, and

Maria had a moustache; Eleni was the looker. I had been amazed that she wanted to marry me.

It was partly pride, that I didn't speak—I wasn't usually secretive. But I kept quiet out of self-preservation, too. It was so painful, to say the words out loud, and once I talked then something would have to happen. One week passed, and another. It was a cool, damp September; she didn't phone. I felt I was sleepwalking.

Costas had lent me the flat above his electrical repair shop, up in London. It was nice of him because he'd only just done it up. It was near to the depot in Peckham and I could walk to work. This was just as well, because Eleni had told me she needed the car, being stuck out in Orpington. I offered to be stuck out in Orpington instead, I loved our house. I told her I'd like us to be stuck out there together, like before, but she wasn't having any of that. So I let her keep the car; if I was nice she might reconsider what she was losing. I even began telling her my trick for starting it in cold weather—it was a seven-year-old Escort and I had tuned up the engine—but then I thought what the hell and put the phone down.

The back of Costas's shop was heaped with microwaves and toasters. They had little tags but most of them were hopeless cases; it was like a hospital down there. Someone had even brought in their kid's remote-controlled police car. One evening I came back with some Kentucky Fried Chicken, I'd had a drink on the way, and I stood looking at it all and realizing it was just useless. I thought of all the things I had bought for our home, sometimes with Eleni beside me, and how by moving my things into the garden she had turned my possessions into junk. It all seemed such a waste. Most of my tools had rusted up but I could never imagine buying any more.

I pictured her lying in the bath, her knees two bumps in the foam, and knew I had never reached her. I knew how her skin felt slippery when she let me dry her, and how frail her shoulderblades were under my hands, and how her shins felt sandpapery when she hadn't shaved them and how she would flinch away and remove my hand to her breast—I knew all this, and how she over-sugared her Shredded Wheat and over-milked my tea, and how she had gripped me sometimes at night with her face averted, and how she collected coupons in garages and then forgot about them—I knew all this and yet, standing in the shop that night, I knew we had never been friends.

* * *

Costas couldn't be a friend, but he was a mate. He took me to the pub a few times but I knew he wanted to be back with his faulty radios or

11

his wife, who was expecting a baby at Christmas. He was expanding the shop and had started a video club; most evenings I took a movie upstairs. I usually read a lot, I liked books, but nowadays it took all my willpower to get through a newspaper.

So I put on a movie instead—they all seemed to have Rod Steiger in them—and then I dozed in front of the TV screen, the way she always said I did. Nowadays she would have some justification, because I wanted to sleep all the time. I stayed up as long as I could, but some nights I gave in at half past nine.

Across the street was the shopping precinct. It was separated from me by the traffic, which hissed in the rain. At night the shop signs glowed and I pinned up a blanket. It was a big concrete precinct with walkways. I fell asleep early but I woke in the small hours. It was then that the man used to shout. He stood outside Mothercare and bellowed; his voice echoed. Sometimes a night bus passed, but nobody lived round here, it was the High Street, and nobody heard him. I tried not to listen; it only seemed a matter of time before I would be joining in.

But most of the time when I lay in bed, waiting for the clock hand to move, I thought about my son.

12

CHAPTER TWO

I had a son, you see, but Eleni cut up his photograph. I'll never forgive her for that. His name was Edward—not a name I would have chosen, but then I hadn't been asked.

There's a certain sort of bloke, when you ask him how many kids he's got he'll say, 'Two, that I know of,' nudge-nudge. 'Two, to my knowledge.' Just so you know he's put it about a bit.

Reg, who ran the depot, he put it about a bit. I had never liked him. The firm was called Peckham Pride Coaches and there were plenty of jokes about the one pecker in Peckham that was always on schedule. I imagine this scene where some socking great twenty-year-old knocks on the office door and Reg says can I help you and the bloke says, 'Hello, Dad.' Or, better still, thumps him on the jaw and says: 'Where the hell have you been all my life?'

There was this chap, when I was a driving instructor, who used to wash the cars. A coloured bloke, I forget his name but he could do a wonderful imitation of Jimmy Saville. Anyway, it was soon after Edward was born and I was feeling low and asked him if he'd got any kids. He said he'd got two with his girlfriend, and his ex-girlfriend had one of his and one of somebody else's, and he had one in

13

Germany, a little girl he'd never seen. I asked how old she would be now and he had to think for ages.

What I mean is, to say I have an illegitimate son gives the wrong impression. I haven't put it about much, at all. For one thing, I hadn't had many girlfriends before I met Eleni. For another, most of them complained that after the first dizzy month or so the whole business seemed to fall off in frequency. They've cited (a) I've gone to sleep while they were still doing their teeth, (b) I've got to a good bit in my book, (c) I've stayed up to watch the Election results come in (well, it's not every day there's a Labour Government, is it?), and (d) I've been going through *Exchange and Mart* to find a new carburettor and by the time I've finished *they'd* gone to sleep.

Once I confided in a bloke at work. 'You know what it's like,' I said, 'when you've got stuck into Dick Francis.' And he said: 'When Frances wants your dick stuck into her.' This might be crude, but it made me laugh. It's a little-known fact, but in the case of *homo sapiens* I've come to the conclusion that after adolescence the female of the species becomes steadily more randy than the male. Except for Reg, but he's hardly human.

*   *   *

I met Lesley back in 1975. Life seemed simpler

in the old days. You could see what a girl's legs were like before you asked her out. Lesley, in fact, was sturdily built but I liked her because she was so interesting. She was my age, thirty, and she'd just given up her secretarial job to study sociology, which people were studying then. I should have seen the danger signs when she went on about women's liberation, but I was only her driving instructor. She was a terrible driver, and I found this endearing when she was so sure about everything else. In fact she was so dangerous that I feared for my life, and this made us close. At the end of our hour, when we shuddered to a halt, we were both sweating.

She said she was an independent woman and needed to take her life into her own hands. I said: what about *my* life? She used to quote me bits out of books. Take a restaurant, she would read. Note how it is the woman's role to listen, to reassure and defer. Yes, I said, and it's the bloke's role to pay. She sighed. All my life women seem to have been sighing at me, and nicking my cigarettes.

She lived in a flat near the Arsenal football ground and in those days I was living nearby. Neither of us knew that area and we were both lonely, though she never let on. She got her friends from the CND because she wanted to ban the bomb and we had some good arguments about that, though I was secretly on her side. But I enjoyed our quarrels; most girls got het up about such petty things, like whether you forgot they liked Bacardi and Coke.

She wasn't that beautiful—she was square, with brown hair—but she always had something new to tell me, even though she embarrassed me in front of her friends by talking about orgasms. She went to a psychiatrist, too, which made her mysterious. She talked about being female as if it was an ailment only she had, and nobody else understood.

Anyway, her lessons were the last in the day so I'd take her for a drink afterwards—did we need that drink!—and then sometimes we went to a film together. I only stayed the night a few times. I remember being touched because despite all her bold talk she was shy, I think she thought she was too beefy, and made me turn the light off.

The day she passed her test she told me she was pregnant. We were sitting in a Wimpy Bar in Hendon, near the Test Centre. I can remember every detail of that place—the manageress dozing, the plastic tomato full of sauce, the sun outside. It was June. I was flooded with love; I jumped up and hugged her.

She sat there, stirring her tea. Her shoulders were wooden.

She said: 'I'm keeping it.'

'Great!' I paused. 'We can get married.'

16

There was a silence. 'You don't understand,' she said.

I sat down opposite her again.

'Of course we can't get married,' she said.

Another pause.

'You needn't feel responsible,' she said, 'just because you're the father.'

'I do feel responsible. I feel wonderful.'

'I mean . . .' She stopped. 'I want this baby, but it's really nothing to do with you.'

At first I thought she was being odd because of her hormones; pregnant women are supposed to be unpredictable, aren't they? She was looking down at her hands; she had stubby fingers, she had bitten her nails right down. Perhaps she didn't want me to feel trapped.

'Desmond,' she said. It's always a danger sign, that. 'Desmond, I'm thirty, I want a child.'

'Same here.'

'I'm talking about me. I want to lead my own life.'

'But what about me?'

'Of course we can't marry. We hardly know each other. We've got nothing in common. You and your cars and pubs and, you know . . . your sort of things.' She inspected her nails but there was nothing left to bite. 'I shouldn't even have told you, but I had to tell somebody. I'm so excited.'

I stared at her. Her brown hair had fallen over her face. 'It's not fair,' I said.

'I wanted one, you see. I'm trying to be upfront, Des.' She moved the plastic tomato, as if that would help. 'We'd better not see each other again.'

There was a pause. I said: 'You just wanted me so you could pass your test.'

'That's not true!'

'No one else would have got you through.'

'Don't be so simplistic,' she said. 'Don't be so male.'

'I am male!' I shouted. 'I'm going to be a father!'

There was a silence. She started stirring her tea again. 'Not really,' she said.

And then she got up and paid our bill.

*   *   *

I only told one person—Eric, who ran the driving school with me. He laughed and said I was a lucky bugger. He said: 'Most birds'd be suing you for paternity.' He hadn't a clue what I was talking about.

Lesley wouldn't see me. She closed ranks, just as Eleni did years later. Women do that; they've always got people on tap. The first time I went round she had an awful woman from the CND there; she was built like a site foreman and she'd never liked me.

The second time her parents were staying. Lesley was hardly on speaking terms with them but there they were, ensconced in her flat and

18

glaring at me as if I was Bluebeard. She was looking pale; she said she'd thrown up outside Boots that morning but she wouldn't let me comfort her. She quarrelled with us all—first me and then her parents—but it was me who was made to leave. On the way home I thought of her feeling sick with our child and got such a stomach ache I had to stop the car.

I tried writing to her. I asked her what was she going to tell the child, would it never know who its father was? She wrote back—short letters with surprisingly childish writing— telling me not to crowd her, not to get heavy, she was quite all right, she could combine having a baby with finishing her studies. She never answered the right questions. She said she'd tell me when the baby was born, but that was it. She sealed the envelopes with *Save the Trees* stickers. I thought: why the hell is she so kind to trees?

When the baby was born, I thought she would see reason. Motherhood changed women, everybody said so. Anyway, when it cried all night she'd want a man around to change its nappies.

By this time, I must say, I couldn't remember how close we had ever been. I certainly couldn't say if I really wanted to marry her. She was right; we hadn't much in common. She had dwindled in my head, back into the distance; she was as unknown as in the first days I'd met her, but changed and hostile

19

and stupidly important. She was a different woman by now—God knows what she thought of me but in a strange way I felt bound to her for life.

In January a letter arrived with the *Save the Trees* sticker. It was stiff; that's because there was a photo inside. It showed a baby, wrapped in a yellow shawl and held by a headless pair of arms. The letter said that here was a photo as promised, it was a little boy and he had been born on January 5 which made him a Capricorn, and that made him harmonious with her as she was Gemini, or something. He was fine and healthy, she was calling him Edward, and she preferred me not to get in touch again, but wished me all the best for the future.

I put the photo in a drawer. My first two thoughts were as clear as crystal. Now, on this earth, I had a son. And that my birthday was in January too, the 19th. I was a Capricorn like him. And that neither he nor his mother would ever know.

And then I went to the pub on the corner, which I'd never gone to because it's Watneys, and for the first time in my life I drank myself under the table.

*   *   *

A few months later the lease expired on the driving school; they were knocking it down to

20

build a Freezer Centre. So I moved away, back to South London where I'd grown up, and I thought that an episode in my life had come to an end.

But in a sense, like Edward, it was just beginning.

CHAPTER THREE

By the time my marriage ended and I was living above Costas's shop, me and my corrugated *Motor Sports*, Edward was eleven. I hadn't seen him, of course. I didn't even know where he lived now. Lesley had never liked North London; she had only stayed for the Polytechnic and she had probably moved on. She had never replied to my letters and I had given up years before. But I still felt a lurch at odd moments, when I read in the paper about a mugging in Highbury, or even when I saw the football results on TV and the name Arsenal appeared. Years before there had been some violence on the pitch and I pictured him living nearby, maybe he had heard the roar. Maybe he had even been taken there. Maybe—he would have been nine then—maybe he liked football and watched the match every Saturday. Perhaps Lesley was married and her husband took him. It caught me unawares, a moment like this, and I felt punched in my

21

chest as if I'd been winded.

You mustn't think I was obsessed. I didn't think about him all the time; I hadn't framed his photo. He was just there. He existed, and sometimes the fact of his existence made my knees weak. I remembered his birthday each year. I couldn't send him anything, of course—I had nowhere to send it to. But I looked in toyshop windows. When he was four I looked at plastic fire engines labelled *2–5 Years* and imagined him pushing one along; when he was seven I saw some Matchbox cars that were much more sophisticated than when I was little, but I had loved them and hoped somebody was buying them for him, though I could never picture who that someone might be. I had only known Lesley; all the people Edward had met since then would be unknown to me. It made him seem separate and experienced, like a foreign child.

I wondered, of course, about his looks. I'm sandy and freckled, and I wondered if he had Lesley's dark hair. Sometimes, just for a moment, I felt like a real father—when I caught myself worrying about his asthma, for instance. I had had it for a few years; it had ended when I was ten, and I wondered if somewhere in Britain he was wheezing, and I longed to tell him that if he was like me it wouldn't last.

I kept pace with his growing-up, at one remove, by looking at other children. I'm an

22

only child so I don't have relations, but I watched my Greek in-laws, and in the early days I stopped at playgrounds and watched the little kids on the swings. I would catch a ball that a boy kicked to me, and ask his mother his age. I watched women zipping up their children's jackets and ticking them off for losing their gloves. It amazed me, that they took their children for granted.

When he was older and I was married and living in Orpington I watched the boys racing down our street on their chopper bikes; it was a great place for kids, trees and gardens and even sort of fields nearby. I'd hear the mothers calling them in to tidy their rooms, usually angrily—why were parents always irritable? It was easy for me, of course. All the same, I envied them their annoyance.

You would think it might fade away, as the years passed; that I'd start to forget him. But I didn't. Funnily enough it grew stronger. I missed him. It was probably because I had no kids of my own. I'd think of the population of London and whether, statistically, I'd bump into him one day in Oxford Street and neither of us would know. Sandy-haired boys caught my attention, but often I'd get their age wrong—it's easy to do that. Sometimes I'd be hired for theatre outings, some pantomime, and I'd stand there helping them down and watching the crowds of kids, boys in red anoraks and blue ones and two-tone ones;

23

boys in school blazers. I just thought about the possibility.

*   *   *

Eleni didn't want children. I hadn't realized that when I married her. The subject hadn't come up—it doesn't really, does it? I had just presumed we would have them one day. In fact, part of her attraction came from her big Greek family. I thought that at last I was connected to something large and fertile, and that she'd want to settle down.

But I hadn't reckoned on her temperament. Soon I realized that in fact she had married me to get out. She wanted to be a dancer and, though she never quite made it, she always thought her big moment was just around the corner. How could she swell up when next week Bernard Delfont might be phoning?

In a sense she was as liberated as Lesley—if liberation means being selfish, which in my bitter moments I decided it did. She was a different sort of person, she did it in a feminine way. She wasn't as clever as Lesley and she was proud of her looks—she was working on her body rather than her mind—but in the end it all boiled down to the same thing: I lost out.

*   *   *

All through September and into October I lay in Costas's flat. As I watched the street lamps glow through my blanket, pinned to the window, I brooded about my life. I suppose I was feeling bitter about everything, even my work which nowadays seemed like a lot of backache at inconvenient hours. I was too tired to be jovial with a bunch of old dears on their day out to Thanet. Why should I? What had they done for me? Them and their endless stops for the toilet. We ran a twice-weekly trip to Boulogne, to the hypermarket, and the shoppers filled me with gloom; they clutched their duty-frees so greedily, as if £2 off was really so important. This worried me; I'm usually sociable. Reg even puts me on the sports runs for the Rotarians, so you can see what I'm like. I thought I might be having a nervous breakdown and I looked at myself cautiously, as if it was happening to somebody else.

I thought that if I had children I'd be doing something better than this. Forty-two and I was still a coach driver. It was a temporary sort of job, working for Reg. All my life I seemed to have been drifting from episode to episode—driving instructor, mini-cab driver, coach driver—and I'd never made up my mind what I really wanted to do. Trouble was, there was nobody to do it for, no young family who'd make me feel constructive. I'd just been biding my time. I should have set up my own driving school, years before—I'd enjoyed doing that and we had built up a lot of custom—but the business with Edward had knocked the wind out of my sails and I'd just taken the first offer that came along, me and my four-door Cortina, which I had then, and that was mini-cabs. I'm probably making excuses, but that's how it seemed and there was nobody there to contradict me. You wind things tighter and tighter, don't you, until you get locked.

October was wet. The buses hissed by and I was living in limbo. I'd worked my way through Costas's repertoire of video films. There was only *The Exterminator* and Kung Fu pictures left and I couldn't face those. Marooned in the high street, surrounded by Safeways and Burtons, I was on an island. Eleni had stolen six years of my life, she'd thrown them into the front garden and stamped on them. Not content with that, she had made a thorough job with the previous years. She had always been incredibly jealous of anyone I'd met before she came along. I'd protested, truthfully, that there hadn't been much and that I loved her more than anybody. But under her C & A sweater beat a fiery Mediterranean heart. I say fiery but now I'd say hysterical. Anyway one day, when I was away at the Edinburgh Tattoo, she cut up all my photos.

It was because I'd told her about Edward. I thought she would understand. I'd just stated the facts: I said it happened years ago, that his

26

mother and I'd had this fleeting thing, and that's what made it so sad—that something so unimportant could create a child. I said that I missed him.

She went quiet. Then, a few minutes later, she jumped up and started to rearrange the furniture. She said she couldn't stand magnolia, we'd got to repaint the lounge, and wasn't Orpington boring, let's move, let's go to Canada. She quite often behaved like this so I didn't get worried. In fact, because I'd told her about Edward and she had appeared to listen, I felt we were closer than usual.

I had this drawer of photos—my parents, who were both dead; me at various stages of childhood, mostly on beaches; snapshots of Continental holidays and various mates' stag nights, that sort of thing. There were one or two girlfriends—giggly ones in a passport photo booth, Polaroids at parties, a nice girl called Gwen whom I took on holiday to the Brecon Beacons—but really not much, considering I was thirty-six when I got married. And, of course, the photo of Edward.

When I came home she told me I had to love her now. When I looked bemused—I'd just driven 450 miles—she opened the empty drawer. She said she'd cut them all up and since then the rubbish men had been. She said: 'Now you can never love anybody but me.'

And that night she burst into tears because I couldn't bring myself to touch her. She was right, in a sense, to cry; because after that night I loved her less.

*   *   *

So I sat in the flat, and it felt like this spring getting tighter round my skull. *It's not fair. How could she do it?* By *she* I didn't just mean Eleni any more; I meant Lesley too, because my old wounds were opened up. They were both women who had done things I couldn't understand. As I squashed my lager cans into the pedal-bin—why was it never big enough?—I thought: I've taught two women to drive. One of them stole my car and the other one stole my son.

*   *   *

One Sunday morning, when I couldn't stand it any more, I phoned Eleni. It was near the end of October and I'd heard nothing from her for a month. I had been imagining so many things that by now I had simply to hear her voice. Perhaps she'd been mulling it over and had decided to have me back; perhaps Maria had persuaded her that at least I was better than most blokes and kept my mortgage repayments up; perhaps I should take her on holiday to Toronto, which for some reason she had always wanted to see, and everything would be all right. Of course there was always

28

the opposite possibility, that she would say something terrible like hadn't I got a solicitor yet? But by now it was worth the risk. Since September I had been sitting beside the phone like a teenager, my heart lurching when it rang; but usually it was somebody asking for Lewisham Discount Carpets because there was something wrong with the line.

Anyway, I dialled my own number—it felt strange, that—and it was engaged. A few moments later I tried again and it was still busy. Eleni liked the phone; if she was complaining about me it was bound to go on for ages. I thought for a moment about money, and how though I didn't have a wife I still had a phone bill, and how unfair it was, that the more she told people how inadequate I was the more I had to pay, and then suddenly I got to my feet, left the flat and took the train to Orpington.

CHAPTER FOUR

It was a twenty-minute walk from the station to my house. It was starting to drizzle and I was having second thoughts. She had often complained that I wasn't spontaneous, but perhaps today wasn't the time to start. Outside the cemetery there was the disabled woman selling flowers, and I thought about buying

29

some. Then I thought bugger me if I'm going to be romantic.

I turned the corner at Thresher Road and walked towards my street. I could smell Sunday dinners cooking; I thought of wives putting on their oven gloves. My waistband was loose; I'd lost weight.

I hadn't shaved that morning and wondered if she would embrace me and then flinch from my stubble, and then decided that if she embraced me I needn't be worrying about that.

I paused at the top of Croxley Road. At the far end, outside my house, I could see our red Escort parked. The place looked blameless. A man whose name I'd never known, who had once helped me push the car, came out of his house and said hello. I wondered if he, or anyone, knew I'd been kicked out. They must have noticed my things in the front garden.

My heart quickened as I walked nearer. And then my front door opened and Eleni came out. She was putting on her coat. She paused, and looked up at the sky, and hurried to the car. I was just about to call out when I saw that she wasn't alone.

A man came out of the house and shut the front door. He double-locked it like a husband. He had a moustache; he zipped up his leather jacket. And then he got into the driving seat of my car and they drove away.

*   *   *

30

You probably think I'd been stupid, not to realize. But I had asked her if she'd fallen for anyone else and she'd said no. She had never been a truthful woman but for some reason I had believed her—I suppose because her list of complaints about me had been so long there didn't seem room for anything else.

I sat on a neighbour's wall for a while, till I felt damp. And then I fished out my keys and went across to my house. I thought: no wonder she hadn't listened when I'd told her about pumping the choke; somebody else was going to start the bleeding car for her.

I let myself into the hose, and paused in the hall. I felt alert; I sniffed the air. I made a swift inspection of the downstairs rooms.

The lounge was spotless. In the kitchen, she had actually done the washing up. It hurt me more than I can say, that the place was so tidy.

I crept upstairs—heavens knows why I crept, when the house was empty. To delay things I went into the bathroom. I wasn't prepared for the scent of her perfume. They're unexpected, scents; they catch you off guard. I paused for a moment. I inspected the basin area; there was his razor, an electric one, on the shelf. Behind the door hung an unknown, blue towelling robe.

I crossed the landing and opened the bedroom door. It smelt airless in there, as if people had been in it for a long time. I stood

31

in the doorway. The room was altered. For a start, she had made the bed. There were turquoise sheets on it too, sheets I'd never seen, and a new patterned duvet cover. The TV had been brought up from the living room and was sitting on the chest of drawers, facing the bed. And there was a bunch of flowers in a vase. She had never put flowers in our bedroom. Perhaps he had put them there. I opened the wardrobe and there were his clothes, hanging next to hers. What a lot of jackets! It wasn't my bedroom any more.

I did a stupid thing, but I needed to do something. I went into the bathroom, unplugged his razor and threw it out of the window, into the shrubbery. It was a puny thing to do, when I felt like chucking his things into the garden, or better still setting fire to the house, but I did it. I didn't want to do something big, or they would know I had been there. Then I took the bottle of scotch from the cabinet in the lounge, let myself out, and caught the train back to London.

*   *   *

That night I phoned Costas. It turned out that he'd known all the time. The man was the ex-husband of somebody at her dancing class. Why hadn't anyone told me? I asked. He said it wasn't his business, it was up to Eleni to tell me in her own time. I put the phone down; I couldn't argue with him when he was lending me his flat. Once you're on your own you have to be nice to people, like a visitor. But I realized then that he wasn't really my mate; at a time like this, despite all their differences, he was still Eleni's brother.

That night, across the road in the shopping precinct, the man started bellowing again. He hadn't been there for weeks. His voice rose like a banshee. The phone rang twice, each time a wrong number. Somebody, stifling his mirth, wanted somebody called Leroy.

I sat down and wrote a letter to Eleni, telling her I wanted a divorce. Then I finished the scotch and smoked about fifty cigarettes. How long had she known him, when had she started lying, when was it exactly that she'd started waxing her legs? I thought of my car, and knew I never wanted to sit in it again. I thought of the bedroom. Ridiculously enough, I would almost have preferred strewn bedclothes, ashtrays, the orgy bit. I'd steeled myself for that. But it had looked so contented. How quickly she'd changed; she had never bothered to be tidy for me. And she had never put flowers beside the bed.

*   *   *

The next morning I had an early run to Luton. My head throbbed and my mouth felt full of ashes. An elderly lady gave me a piece of

Toblerone but it didn't do the trick, not at 6.30. My passengers were going to Majorca and I had a sudden urge to dump the coach at the airport and go with them, but then I'd always have to come back again, wouldn't I, some time or another?

There was only one person amongst them under fifty; she was a big girl, with glasses. As I unloaded the luggage she leant towards me and whispered: 'Trust me to go and get cystitis.' Now what did that mean? What were women up to?

The Monday rush hour had started; traffic was thick. I drove down the M1, back towards London, with fifty-three empty seats behind me. I switched on the radio. I thought that my wife's boyfriend couldn't have a shave that morning, and how bad behaviour spreads. I thought that somewhere in England my son might be getting ready for school. I wished my parents were still alive. My brains felt as if they were boiling and when I looked at my hands on the wheel they belonged to somebody else. I wondered if I was unhinged and if they would take away my licence. The windscreen wipers slewed to and fro; behind me a lorry flashed its lights. I remembered watching *Porridge* on TV; the prisoners discussing how some geezer got three years for stealing a car while somebody else only got one year for manslaughter, and Ronnie Barker said no wonder when it takes twenty minutes to make a car and only five

34

minutes to make a person. I tried to work this out and found I was laughing out loud, a high noise that frightened me. I wondered if I should pull onto the hard shoulder for a moment. Perhaps I was ill.

What happened next sounds small; after all, it only meant turning the wheel. I was approaching Hendon. Instead of driving straight on, which led to Hendon, and then to Swiss Cottage, and then the West End, and then Stockwell, and then, eventually, to Peckham and the depot—instead of behaving as per usual, sound in wind and limb and brain—instead I indicated left. Two cars hooted, I cut across the slow lane, another lorry blared its horn and I was on the A1 dual carriageway, crawling east amongst the traffic which moved with me towards Finchley, and then Holloway, and on to Arsenal, until an hour later—well, it was the rush hour—I was inching my coach down the street I hadn't set foot in for eleven years.

*   *   *

Ardley Street had tall terraced houses with butchered plane trees in front of them. It had stopped raining. I'm superstitious. When I saw a parking space long enough for my coach, opposite number 46, Lesley's old place, my stupid spirits rose. I turned off the engine, turned off the radio, sat there and smoked a cigarette.

It was 9.15. I narrowed my eyes until the doorway blurred; I saw the door opening and a boy hurried out, carrying a satchel and a pair of football boots.

But he was too late for school, and I was too late by years, far too late. I knew that, of course.

Number 46 had been smartened up. Last time I'd been here, eleven years before, it was a tacky place divided into flats—concrete out front, dustbins and a broken motorbike, all that. Now it was painted white; there were blinds at the windows and tubs in the garden, still filled with last summer's geraniums, and somebody had parked a Range Rover on the hard standing.

I thought of Lesley's light glimmering in the ground floor flat, and her Hyde Park Rally poster in the window. I took out another cigarette, and then put it back in the packet. I climbed down from the coach and went across the road.

There was only one bell now; this was a family house. The door was opened by a woman with a scrubbed, creamy face. She looked at me politely.

'I'm looking for somebody called Lesley Featherstone,' I said. The name sounded clumsy; I hadn't spoken it for so long. 'Who used to live here.'

'Gosh,' she replied. 'We've only just moved

in.' Behind her a baby was crawling along the floor like a caterpillar. 'Naughty!' she cried. 'Naughty Abby.' She picked it up and turned to me. 'Lesley? Never heard of him.'

'Her,' I said. 'It's a woman.' At the back of the hall I could see paint pots and a ladder.

'We only moved in this year and we bought it from people called Lebovitz.' She frowned. 'I'm sure she was called Bettina.'

'She lived here. She really did.'

The baby squirmed in her arms. She said: 'Before then I think it was flats and God knows who they all were.'

My head ached. I pointed down the hallway, then I said clearly: 'I had a son in there.'

'Sorry?' She was gazing at me.

I cleared my throat. It hadn't sounded right. Instead I said: 'No sun this year.'

The words still sounded wrong. She smiled at me, puzzled, and, said: 'Ghastly, isn't it.' She gestured at the sky, with her free hand. 'This time next week I'll be in Tenerife.'

*   *   *

I went back to the coach. The words I'd spoken to that woman worried me; I hadn't sounded like myself.

It was stupid, of course, to have come. It was only because I'd finished work for the day—that's what I told myself. I strolled down to the end of the street. Too much time had

37

passed; the whole place had gone upmarket. The Volvo squad had moved in. Years ago it was kids and radios playing; at night it was like walking through *West Side Story*. But the kids had grown-up and the people had gone, long ago. Today the street was silent with money. And when I got to the end I found they'd closed it off and called it an Environmental Area, so I'd have to back the blooming coach out.

*   *   *

When I approached the coach a man came out of a nearby house, one of the few scruffy ones, and stood looking at me. Beside him stood, on bowed legs, one of the plainest dogs I've ever seen.

'Shouldn't be here,' he said, jerking his head up at my coach. 'Should be down there.' He jerked his head the other way. 'There's a coach park, for you lot. They'll be relieving themselves in my bleeding hedge.'

He paused for breath. I heard his dog wheezing.

'I'm not taking anyone to the match,' I said. 'Honest.' I was going to add that it was Monday and there was no football today anyway, but he didn't look receptive. Instead I said: 'Actually I'm looking for a little boy.'

'Lost a passenger?'

I shook my head and pointed to the house

38

opposite, number 46. 'I don't suppose you remember a little boy lived there, when they were flats? He lived on the ground floor, with his mother, years ago.'

The man nodded. There was a silence.

I stared at him. 'You do?'

He nodded again.

'A little boy,' I said, 'and his mother was called Lesley.'

'The lady with the hat.'

I paused. I'd forgotten about her hat. She had worn this bobble-hat, a purple knitted thing, right up to the summer. It hadn't done a lot for her looks—with the dungarees she'd resembled a carpenter's apprentice—but I hadn't known her well enough to hint at that. Come to think of it, you never know women well enough to hint at it.

'What was the little boy like?' I asked. 'When did they move? Do you know where they went?'

He shook his head. 'They was flats then, but they're not getting me out.' He paused; his dog sneezed. 'I'm staying put.'

'Did anyone else know her?'

'Who?'

'The lady with the hat?'

He didn't reply. His dog sneezed again. A moment earlier I'd felt fond of his dog but I'd gone off them both now. Neither of them was listening.

I tried once more. 'Did she have any friends

39

here?'

'Just Pam.'

'Pam?'

'You know Pam.'

'I don't know anyone.'

He wiped his nose. 'She had this little kid too.'

'Where does she live?'

'She's gone now.' He jerked his head at his house. 'She lived on the top floor but they're not getting rid of me.'

'You don't know how I could find her?'

He looked at me. 'You from the council?'

I shook my head.

'Oh no,' he said. 'You drive them hooligans.'

'You don't know where Pam's gone?'

He shook his head. There was a smell of exhaust and a surge of pop music; a lorry was inching past my coach. It was carrying a skip, for one of the houses being done up.

'She was a dentist, see,' he said.

'A dentist?'

'Pint-sized little thing, but then she was Australian.'

'She's gone to Australia?'

'Oh no,' he said testily. 'Tottenham.'

'How do you know?'

'She's a dentist. She had all these letters after her name.'

'What letters?'

'It's on her card.'

'What card?'

40

'What do you mean, what card?' He glared at me. 'The card in the hall.'

I've always wanted to be a private detective. A moment later there I was, pencil at the ready, standing in his hallway inspecting the cards pinned up for mini-cabs and emergency plumbers, and amongst them one for P.K. Johnson, BDS, LCS, Dental Surgeon, and an address just a mile away, in N.17.

CHAPTER FIVE

It wasn't a dentist's, it was a sex shop. I thought: what a mug I am.

It was a modern row of shops next to a housing estate. Most of the shops had grilles over the windows; this one, Private Shop, had knickers displayed and things on boxes that I didn't look at too closely. I glimpsed a label saying *Swedish Tickler*. I thought: what a wally. I suppose I am a bit dozy; in pubs I don't always get the jokes. Pam's card was for another sort of service altogether. Women were always putting those cards up, I saw them in phone boxes—*Strict French Lessons*, they said, and *Mahogany Polishing*. What worried me was what BDS, LDS stood for. A man of forty-two, I should know. In my experience there wasn't a lot you could do with teeth, but I was obviously wrong. No wonder I hadn't been able to keep a wife.

A woman passed, pushing a pram, and glared at me. I moved away and then I saw the door, and the *Surgery* bell, and I looked up and on the first-floor window it said *Dental Surgeon.*

I rang the bell and a disembodied voice let me in. Upstairs was a waiting room. There was only one person in it, a boy who was crying.

I sat down beside him. 'It's not that bad,' I said.

He didn't reply; he was blowing his nose.

'When I was a nipper,' I said, 'when I was your age, it was like a road drill.' I made the noise, loudly. 'Don't know how lucky you are.'

He still didn't reply.

'Honest,' I said, 'it's nothing to cry about.'

'I'm not crying,' he said. 'I've got a cold.'

I paused. His eyes were red.

He pointed to the surgery door. A whine came from it. 'I'm waiting for my Mum.'

'I see.'

'Sodding hell, I'm bored.'

He shouldn't have sworn, at his age. I said: 'She won't be long.'

'She'll be all bloody morning.'

'Blimey. What's she having done?'

He looked at me as if I was three years old. 'She's the frigging dentist.'

I paused. 'She's Pam?'

He nodded. 'Finished my *Mads.*' He pointed to his comics. 'And she's got a lousy selection

42

of magazines. All women's crap.'

'Shouldn't you be at school?'

'Got this cold, haven't I?'

The room was silent; the whine had stopped. I looked at the boy, who was picking his fingernails with a matchstick, and my stupid heart thumped.

I said: 'How old are you?'

He looked at me as if I should know. 'Eleven and three-quarters.'

All of a sudden a strange thing happened. He was no longer a rude kid with a runny nose; he had changed into a precious child. This was the boy who had played with my son. He knew more about my son than I did. I watched him, awe-struck. From his pocket he drew out a damp length of toilet paper and blew his nose.

I took a breath but my tongue wouldn't work properly: 'You know about Edward!' I said loudly.

He gazed at me for a moment; then thank goodness the surgery door opened and a man came out, followed by a small, ruddy woman in a Doctor Kildare tunic. The man went downstairs.

She looked at me and said in an Australian twang: 'You're not Mrs Patel.'

'No.'

She shrugged. 'She's always late.'

I didn't know what to do next, so I shook her hand. 'I'm Desmond.'

43

'Pleased to meet you, Desmond.' She grinned. Unlike most dentists she had a terrific set of teeth.

I didn't know where to start, so I just said: 'I've come about Lesley.'

She frowned for a moment. Then she said: 'Oh yes. She's coming at three.'

My stomach lurched. I paused. 'Lesley is?'

She nodded. 'She really needs to see an orthodontist. Maybe you can persuade her.' She gave a pile of dental wipes to her son, who blew his nose. 'You her stepdad?'

I paused for a moment. 'No,' I said. 'I mean Lesley Featherstone.'

'Featherstone?'

'Lesley, of Ardley Road.'

'Lesley, of *Ardley Road*!'

I nodded.

'Miss Castration Complex!'

'Pardon?'

'Miss Penis Envy!' She laughed. 'Boy, did that woman have hang-ups.'

'Did she?'

'Men the oppressors, all that shit. Germaine Greer's got a lot to answer for, even if she is an Ozzie. You knew her?'

'Didn't she write a book?'

'Did she?' She looked surprised.

'The female something.'

She paused. 'Not Greer, nitwit. Lesley. You a friend of hers?'

'No,' I said. 'Yes. Not really.'

44

She took one of the dental wipes and blew her nose. Then she said to her son: 'I'm catching your frigging cold.' She turned back to me. 'Lucky you caught me. Next month we're going back to Sydney.'

I nearly said 'Who's he?' but I stopped. There was something wrong with my brain that morning.

She went on: 'I've had enough of this lousy country, no offence, but look at it.'

She stood at the window. It was starting to rain again; the ground-floor flats opposite had been boarded up. Down below there was a Mercedes parked.

'See that Merc?' she said. 'That's my landlord.' A man came out of the sex shop and got into the car. 'Mrs Thatcher's Britain, it stinks. I want my son to have some sort of a life.'

The boy said: 'Mercs are wik.'

'What's wik?' I asked.

'Wicked,' he said patiently. 'What car've you got?'

I was going to say an Escort but I stopped. 'A coach.'

'A coach!' For the first time he looked his age. He pressed his face against the window. The front half of the coach was jutting out of the council estate car park: big and shiny; two-tone bodywork, green and cream.

'It's not exactly mine.'

'Wik!'

45

'Tell me about Lesley,' I said, sitting down on a chair.

Her son went off to buy another comic. She sat down beside me.

'Boy, was she screwed-up.'

'Was she?' I felt a tweak of relief. Perhaps it hadn't been all my fault.

'She used to sit in my room for hours going on about gender bias at college, and how it was a patriarchal syllabus, and how in conversation male dominance to female was 70 to 30.'

I smiled. That sounded familiar.

She grinned. 'So I told her she was sure making up for the 30.' She paused. 'We had some laughs, she was all right when you got her off her hobby-horse. She was just incredibly fierce about men. I think she had some problem there but I never knew what it was.' She took another dental wipe. 'Christ knows what it'll do to her son.'

'Edward.'

'That's it, Edward.' She spoke the name carelessly; I'd never heard a stranger speak it. *Edward* filled the waiting room.

'Edward,' I repeated. Then I asked: 'What do you mean? Wasn't she a good mother?'

She sighed. 'Who is? It's the hardest job in the world.'

'Is it?'

'You got kids?'

'Sort of.' I paused. 'Wasn't she bringing him up properly?'

46

'Do I bring up Butler properly? Who knows?'

'But Edward . . .' I felt like the anxious father I had never been.

'I'm just saying, it's hard on your own.' She grimaced. 'But then again it's hard with someone else.'

'She didn't have to be on her own!' I blurted out.

She looked at me curiously. 'You a relative or something?'

'Not really,' I said. 'I just wanted to see her . . . Talk about old times.'

'Haven't seen her for yonks. Seven years.'

'Where did she go?'

She picked up her son's toilet paper and took it to the bin. 'Lancaster,' she said. 'No, Leicester.'

'Leicester?'

'She joined some women's thing.'

'What sort of women's thing?'

'Some shared house, I think. I've probably got the address.'

She went into the surgery. I heard her saying 'Where's my frigging Filofax?' The phone rang and somebody answered it; the buzzer went.

I sat there gazing at a poster saying *What Is This Thing Called Plaque?* I felt a peculiar sensation. It was as if I had put a blank square of photographic paper into some developing fluid and a picture was starting to appear,

47

fuzzy and vague.

The door opened and a lady arrived, wearing a sari with an overcoat on top. Pam came out of the surgery to greet her; she looked brisk now.

She opened her address book. 'Forbes, Fitch,' she said, scanning the Fs. 'Foyles Bookshop, why did I ever want that? Featherstone. 12, Talbot Close, Leicester. No phone number.' She closed the book. 'Must go.'

'Wait!'

'What?'

I took a breath. 'Was Edward . . . I mean . . .'

'What?'

'Was he a nice child?'

She smiled. Then she nodded. 'Absolutely gorgeous.'

*　　　*　　　*

Down the far end of the shops there was a newsagent's. I paused outside. It was then that I made up my mind not to go back to Peckham that day. I thought: what the heck.

I went in and bought a copy of *Mad*, for my son. And then I picked up a *Beezer* book, because I used to love that when I was eleven. But then I decided that I was too superstitious to buy the whole book at £2.95. It wasn't the money; it was the hope.

So I bought a *Beezer* comic instead, at 20p,

and went back to the coach. A watery sun had come out; on the pavement, the broken glass glinted. I realized I was whistling *What is this thing called love?* I wished Pam luck in Australia. I felt reckless and light-headed, but I convinced myself it was only because I was skiving.

It was back to the M1 for me. In an hour and a half I would be in Leicester. *This funny thing called love . . .* I put the engine into first and squeezed the coach past the parked cars towards the end of the street. I was just turning into the main road when somebody sneezed.

*   *   *

I jammed on the brakes. The noise had come from behind me. A car hooted and I pulled into a bus stop. Far back in the coach I heard a rustle.

Some kids from the housing estate must have got in; God knows what they'd do to Reg's upholstery.

I walked to the end of the coach. Another sneeze. Somebody was crouching on the floor. I grabbed the legs and pulled.

It was Butler.

'What on earth are you doing here?'

'I want to come with you,' he said.

'Don't be silly.'

He sniffed. 'I'm bored.'

49

'Bored? At your age?'

'It's boring.'

'What is?'

'Everything.'

Boys shouldn't talk like this. He sprawled on the seat. I looked at his blotchy face.

'I was never bored when I was eleven,' I said.

'Well, I am.'

'That's not the way for a child to talk!' I said. 'There's lots of things to do.'

'What?'

'Well. Bikes and . . . football . . .' I gestured around. People waiting for the bus gazed up at us through the windows. 'Trees to climb . . .'

'Oh yeah?'

'Stuff like that.'

'There's nothing to sodding do.'

'Don't swear!'

He stared at me. His nose was running. I looked at him with distaste. With a jolt I wondered: would I actually like my son? Absolutely gorgeous, Pam had said. Could she be trusted? Could Edward be trusted now?

The coach darkened; a bus had double-parked beside us. The queue shuffled past; some of them glared up at us.

'Anyway, soon you'll be in Australia.'

For the first time, he brightened. 'Dad's in Australia.'

'You've got a Dad?'

'Course.'

50

'Some people haven't.'

He looked at me as if I were a backward pupil. 'Everyone's got a Dad.'

* * *

I gave him the *Beezer*. He said it was a kid's comic, but he took it. I drove him back to the surgery and half an hour later I was on the M1 and the huge, blue, hopeful sign said *Midlands and The North*.

CHAPTER SIX

Music was another thing that had annoyed my wife. My music, of course. But why shouldn't I like Brian Poole and the Tremeloes? I felt safe, with Brian.

I blamed it on her age. She chortled over my Beatles photos; 'The Fab Four!' she whinnied. 'Look at those trousers!' Secretly I admitted that by now they did look funny, but it was a funniness I had been through and I prickled with loyalty for them. Eleni was ten years younger than me. I would forget that for a while, but music jolted us apart a decade. Some of it was jealousy. She thought all that free love and flower power meant I'd had a good time. I told her, truthfully, that growing up in the sixties was like hearing a party in the next room. So then she called me a fuddy-duddy. You can't win.

I felt free in the car. I could play my tapes there. When you look at a traffic jam it seems senseless, miles of men bumper to bumper when it's quicker by train. But I bet they're all married. I had the cream of my cassettes in the Escort; I felt bitter about that, of course, and had demanded them back. I also had a few at the depot, which I'd bring with me in whatever vehicle I was driving. Eleni might sneer, but it can't help lifting your spirits to hear a coachload of over-sixties singing along to Herman's Hermits. There was always one brave soul who tries the harmonies.

That Monday I had just brought two tapes with me—*Ricky Nelson Hits* and *The Definitive Shadows*. After all, I had only planned on a trip to Luton. I slotted in Ricky and thought about Butler. Why had he disturbed me? He was the wrong boy in my coach, true. But I wondered if I would ever find the right one.

For start, I might never find him at all. Seven years ago my son had been taken to Leicester. Could I rely on him still being there? Nobody stayed put any more; my son's life was as unreliable as anyone else's.

Since my young day, the world had changed. John Lennon had been shot, pubs bleeped to video games and wives invited strange men under their duvets. Edward was growing up in a treacherous world and in an odd way he knew it better than I did, because until that September I had felt safe.

Marriage was for keeps, I thought. Marriage meant staying together, like my parents did, and raising a child. Mothers knitted. You opened the door to the smell of cooking.

Nobody thought about doing their own thing—like dyslexia, the word hadn't been invented. My parents would have found such talk baffling and selfish. Lesley's complaints would never have entered their heads; Mum had never hankered for Toronto.

These last few weeks I'd been realizing that the world had changed. Like Rip Van Winkle I was waking up. The spray sparkled on the motorway and I realized I was travelling into another England, my son's England, and that despite being forty-two I was more innocent, for better or worse, than he could ever be. Wherever he lived.

I thought that I might not find him. And then I thought: what would happen if I did? In my daydreams he had been a sandy-haired boy, full of beans; he had been my ideal son. I suppose he was myself at eleven. But daydreams are easy. Easy to be a father when you've never been one. Butler hadn't been easy. I'd only known him half an hour and I had nearly thumped him.

I decided not to think—not yet. *Hello, Mary Lou*, sang Ricky. *Goodbye heart.* My spirits rose. I was taking a day off, and I deserved it. I

53

stopped at Watford Gap and filled up the coach with diesel.

One of the phones was working so I rang Costas's shop and told him not to worry if he didn't see my light that evening, I hadn't done myself in. I don't think he understood, because he replied: 'Attaboy, you lucky sod. Glad you're perking up.'

Then I found the estate agent who had sold us Croxley Road and told them to put it on the market. I pictured Eleni opening the door to a man holding one of those laser guns they use to measure rooms. She'd think they had come to shoot her.

It was lunch time. I ate a large plate of sausage and chips and watched a lorry-driver chat up his hitchhiker. She must have been Dutch because she rolled him a cigarette. Dutch girls smoke all the time; I'd seen them on my Bulb Weekends.

She lit it for him, which made her look tender, and I wished him luck. I wished everybody luck. Life was so chancy, it made my mind reel. Here we were, me and my Volvo Elite III Panorama coach, halfway up the M1 and all because of a dentist's card. These sausages would never have been eaten by me. Edward was a dirty great eleven-year-old, he knew how to switch channels and tie his laces, he'd eaten at least eight flavours of crisps, and all because of a moment's fumbling in the dark.

Perhaps he was dead.

*   *   *

Back in the coach I told myself again that this was just a jaunt and nothing would come of it. Does your mood change after a meal? After my chips I felt measured and cautious. I drove in the slow lane. I wanted to savour this drive, because I didn't have a clue what I would find at the end.

They had moved away. She had married and gone to live in Toronto—no, Peebles, Hull, Hounslow. Minnesota. She had formed a lesbian attachment and taken him to a commune in Strathclyde. She had been killed in a road accident and he had gone to live with a maiden aunt who believed in an afterlife. He had been fostered with Filipinos. She had become an eminent sociologist. She had joined the Hare Krishnas—I wouldn't put anything past her—and he had become a pasty-faced child who wanted to save my soul.

The sun had dried the motorway. I slotted in The Shadows and Hank's guitar weaved its magic. She had married and he called her husband Dad. Dad did all the things I had never been able to do. He helped him with his maths and when he washed the car he let his son—my son—polish the wheels. When he bought his paper *(Mirror? Guardian?* Perhaps even the *Daily Express,* who knows?), he

55

bought him football stickers as a surprise; I'd seen kids of Edward's age squabbling over those in newsagents'.

It pained me, but I imagined them as parents, this blurred couple, Lesley and this man, and as they grew clearer I realized they were starting to resemble my own parents, proper parents, fixed ones, and that the little boy, despite his knowledge of current TV programmes, was me. As he always had been.

*   *   *

I nearly missed the turning. I was too busy dreaming things up. My cigarette packet slid as I slewed off to the left. Cars had been hooting at me all day. This hurt; about the only thing I'm good at is driving. Even my wife hadn't complained about that.

It was 2.30 when I drove into Leicester. I realized, with surprise, that it was only a few hours since I'd been sitting at Luton Airport. I seemed to have been driving for weeks.

CHAPTER SEVEN

I had never been to Leicester. I drove round the Ring Road and pulled into a lay-by. I took out the large-scale map of Britain; it had Town Street Plans in it and searching through

Leicester I found Talbot Road. It was near the centre. Talbot Close, I guessed, wouldn't be far away.

I sat for a moment. The sun glinted on the windows of the semis which lined the Ring Road. A solid row of cars was parked in front of them. When I was young hardly anyone had a car.

I tilted the driving mirror. My eyes were still bloodshot from my alcoholic night. I noticed for the first time how deep the grooves were, that ran from my nose to the corners of my mouth. Age had crept up on me. My wrinkles were like the number of cars on the roads. For years I hadn't noticed anything; now, because I'd had a jolt, I saw how many had arrived on the scene. A child grows older with its father; they do it together. In Edward's case it was different. If I found him, here in Leicester, he would be faced with Instant, Ready-Cooked middle-age. I started the engine. Then I stopped it, and combed my hair.

*   *   *

Half an hour later I was easing my coach into Talbot Close. It was where I had guessed. I parked near the corner. It was a narrow cul-de-sac. Small, terraced houses ended in a monster school that blocked off the sun. My heart was knocking against my ribs, it seemed to have a life of its own.

I walked up to number 12. It was one of the smarter ones, painted cream. There was a piece of paper pinned to its door.

I hesitated. My armpits were damp. What if somebody was watching from a window?

Something touched my leg. I jumped. It was a cat. I knelt down and stroked its arched, shivering back. It pressed against my ankles, and that made me feel welcome.

I crossed the road. I thought, if this were a dream the note would say *Hi, Dad, long time no see.* I stepped nearer. Of course it didn't. It said: *Fulton Furnishings: Back at 4.15.* I looked at the writing. Could it be Lesley's? It was printed carefully, in biro, on a page torn out of an exercise book. It could have been a schoolboy's book.

I looked up. *Some women's thing,* Pam had said, *Some shared house.* It was only two storeys high, but the sort of women who shared might like to be squashed together, close. The note meant that nobody was at home.

I couldn't see anything through the ground-floor window; the curtains were closed. So I bent down, pushed open the letter box and peered in.

I could see a hallway. Inside, leaning against the wall, was a bike. It was one of those Choppers. It had some stickers on it, flash ones in silver. No question: a boy's bike.

I felt stung. I moved back quickly and

58

walked down the road. I smoothed back my hair; my palms were damp. I stood beside the school gates, collecting my wits.

He still lived there. That bike belonged to an eleven-year-old. There was a slim chance it might be another eleven-year-old, but for some reason I felt confident. I can only say that it looked like the sort of bike my son would have; it just did. I'd had a bike at his age—not a Chopper of course, they weren't invented, but it was flash for its era. I had painted it gold and spent six weeks' pocket money on its bell. That bike was the beginning of my love affair with anything on wheels.

Back at 4.15. Did that mean Lesley? Now I had seen her street she had grown so possible that I felt like hiding. I pictured her coming round the corner; she wore her old army coat and bobble-hat and she fished for her door-keys. She would have changed her clothes since then, of course; what did women like her wear now?

Back at 4.15. It might be one of the sharing women who would be coming back then. Actually, I would prefer that. I could announce myself at one remove and spare everybody a heart attack. On the other hand, it could be Edward, back at 4.15 after school. His careful printing.

I looked at my watch. 3.20. Just then I heard a child shouting.

'Wait!' it cried.

I swung round.

'Hey, wait!'

I peered through the railings. A child was hurrying across the playground. He wasn't running towards me, of course; he was catching up with two boys who were going into a Portakabin. I decided to wait it out, at the school gates. School would end at 4.00. If he lived in this street, then this was likely to be his school. *Boys and Girls 11–18 Yrs* said its sign. I took out a cigarette and lit it. In the building a bell rang.

For an absurd moment I felt like an ordinary father on an ordinary day. An ice-cream van had moved into position nearby. Children crossed the playground. Many of them were brown, and some wore turbans. They jostled each other; one shouted, 'Fuck off, Ahmed!' There was a banner at one of the windows but from here I couldn't read it. I hadn't been near a school for a quarter of a century, not since I'd been at my own, St Botolph's High in Bromley. It had been surrounded by trees which in my memory were always in full leaf. *Oh come all ye faithful* we sang in the hall. There had only been one black boy; he had bragged, untruthfully, that he was a prince.

3.35. The last lesson must be in progress. Pupils, however, still seemed to be wandering around. Two girls, in tight skirts, leant against the Portakabin, popped something into their

60

mouths and dropped the paper. Nobody wore school uniform; it gave the place a casual, adult air, as if the pupils had just decided to visit for an hour or two. They looked older than I remembered.

Behind me the ice-cream man hawked and spat. On a normal day I would have chatted to him. The sun had gone in. Two women strolled up—mothers coming early. They were talking about marg and butter. Then I realized it was somebody called Marg who wasn't speaking any more to somebody called Betty.

In the playground the two girls were exchanging shoes. I heard their giggles. A chill breeze was blowing; from some building behind the school I heard a faint tannoy. I smoothed down my hair and smoked another cigarette. One of the women said: 'So they told him he had polyps in his throat.' I wondered whether I'd remembered to lock the coach.

3.41. I felt blank. I suppose it was the shock; I hadn't caught up with myself yet. Now I was standing here, I felt numb. Funnily enough it reminded me of my wedding day, standing with a vague hangover, telling myself I must feel something quickly, some intense emotion, because in a moment it would be over and they'd turf us out of the registry office. In the coach it had been natural to dream about Edward, and imagine what he would look like. Now I was here I didn't even know what to say. How would I recognize him? I would just

61

watch which boy walked down to number 12.

I shivered, and fastened up the neck of my anorak. A few more women had joined the group now. I almost felt familiar with my original two, who were talking about somebody called Oonagh and how they knew she wouldn't bring back the videotape. I thought that of course I wouldn't buy anything like an ice-cream, but the van was there for later, and if it was gone there was always the corner shop. And then I made up my mind and hurried across to the shop—it was just the downstairs room in the last house, really, and with hardly anything on the shelves, it wasn't like London here—and bought him a packet of Rolos and a Mars Bar. It was 3.52.

*   *   *

I was just coming out when somebody stepped up to me. I moved out of her way, to let her through the door, but she grabbed my shoulder.

'I live here,' she said. She had a strong Leicester accent; for a moment I couldn't understand her. With her free hand she pointed at one of the houses. 'I live in that house and I've been watching you,' she looked at her watch. 'For an hour.' She took a breath. 'And I've been reading my evening paper recently.'

I thought she must be talking to somebody

else, but there was nobody behind me.

'I said I've been reading my paper. Know something? You're quite a celebrity by now.'

'What?'

'I saw you—buying those sweeties.'

The women at the gates had turned and were gazing at us. I cleared my throat.

'You going to pretend otherwise?' She demanded. Over her apron she was wearing an overcoat in a horrible shade of maroon. She took another breath. 'Now you're going to tell me you're a father here.'

'I am!'

'Who are you waiting for?'

'Well, sort of.'

'Sort of, he says.' She drew a breath; there was perspiration on her forehead. Everyone was silent, listening. 'Men like you, you're worse than animals, you're—'

'Edward Featherstone!'

'What?'

'I'm waiting for a boy called Edward Featherstone!' I cried.

'And what class is he in?'

'He's in . . .' I stopped. 'I don't know.'

'He doesn't know!'

'He's eleven.'

'Getting younger, aren't they. You pervert, you—'

I shouted: 'He lives here!'

I pulled her round so we were facing down the road. 'He lives in number twelve!'

I looked at the cream house. Something had changed. For a moment I couldn't work out what it was, and then I realized: the paper was no longer on the door.

I pushed the woman away and hurried down the street. Outside number 12 I paused for a moment to catch my breath. Then I rang the bell.

*　　　*　　　*

The door opened. A tall Indian man stood there. I stared at him. He smiled back.

'Good afternoon,' he said. 'You have the sofabed?'

I shook my head. There was a pause. Far away I heard the school bell ring; at the same moment, the ice-cream van started playing a melody. I thought: perhaps that woman has called the police.

'Do you live here?' I asked.

He nodded. 'Something has happened to it?'

'No. I was just wondering about the bike.'

'I beg your pardon.'

The bike, there.' I pointed into the hall. In the gloom, a woman and a child were peering at me.

'The bicycle?' he asked.

'I thought it belonged to my son.' That wasn't quite what I meant to say; he wouldn't understand.

'You are saying that my son has taken your son's bicycle?'

'No!' I cried. 'Sorry.' I took a breath. He was still looking at me kindly. 'I made a mistake. I'm looking for the people who used to live here. A little boy called Edward.'

'Edward?'

I nodded. He gazed at me politely. His wife had come nearer; the child peered from behind her.

'The people before you, was there a boy called Edward?'

He shook his head, turned and said something to his wife. Perhaps that he had a loony here. He turned back. 'My wife reminds me. The previous tenants, they had two charming little girls.'

I didn't know what to say next. Down the road I heard the whoops and shouts of the children coming out of school. The woman must have been bluffing, about the newspaper, or I'd be hearing the sirens by now.

The man was still standing there kindly, waiting for me to speak. His wife whispered something to him. She was one of the most ravishing women I had ever seen.

'Maddy and Janie,' he said.

'What?'

'The two little girls.'

'How long have you been here?'

'We have lived here a year,' he replied.

'And the people before?'

He was still polite, but it couldn't go on for ever. 'I don't know. Perhaps for two or three years.'

At that point a boy came up, swinging a carrier bag.

'This is my son, Salim,' said the man.

'Hello,' said the boy. To my amazement he already had black down on his upper lip.

There was a pause. Behind us the street was full of schoolchildren. I couldn't think what to do next. The man's wife whispered to him again; in her foreign language. She was probably telling him to get rid of me.

In despair I said: 'Is there nobody who'd know? Who'd lived here—oh, seven years ago?'

'There's Mrs Selwyn,' said the boy.

'Who's Mrs Selwyn?'

He pointed to the next-door house, number 10. 'She told me she'd lived here since she was a girl.'

'Is she in?'

The boy shook his head. 'She's gone.'

'Gone?'

'She lives at that place now.'

'What place?' I asked.

The woman said something to her husband. I've often wondered why it takes twice as long when people aren't speaking English. I didn't like this street any more and knew I should admit defeat.

The man turned to me. 'She lives in the

Sheltered Housing.'

'Where's that?'

The boy pointed. 'Left at Talbot Road, on past the market and first street on the right.'

'Thanks.' On impulse, I gave him the paper bag. He took out the Mars Bar and Rolos. 'For you,' I said.

I felt warmer towards the street now. I gazed up at the house, remembering it for Edward. Whatever had happened since, this street had once been familiar to him. We could share that memory, anyway.

I was just about to leave when a man came up. He carried a piece of paper.

'Mr Ibrahim Mohammed?' he said.

'Mohammed Ibrahim,' corrected the Indian man.

'Oh well, same thing.' He looked at the paper again. 'One English Honeysuckle Sofabed.'

'Yes.' He looked around. 'Where is it?'

The man pointed up the street. 'Can't get the van in. Some dickhead's parked his coach on the corner.'

*   *   *

At the market I got stuck in a traffic jam. The place was just packing up; people were dismantling stalls and loading up double-parked vans. My vehicle didn't help and I got some dirty looks. I ignored them. I was still

67

upset by the woman in the maroon coat calling me a pervert. Women had called me a lot of things: 'insensitive' (Eleni), 'boring' (Eleni), 'undersexed' (Eleni), 'drunk' (a girl I met at a party) and, most hurtful of all, simply 'male' (Lesley), but nobody had ever called me a pervert. She had said it with such hatred it had seemed like glee. It was so unfair when I was not only waiting for my son but he hadn't been there anyway. *Women*, I thought.

I sat there, the engine idling. I wasn't in a hurry anyway, because I didn't hold out much hope for this Mrs Selwyn. Ahead of me was a Transit van. A purple-faced man in a sheepskin coat was loading up pieces of pale, lolling tripe; I realized it was foam. To my right, a Pakistani chap was packing loo-rolls and toothpaste into boxes. There was a meat stall with a sign above it in Hindi or something. Its chickens were wizened and yellow, not like English ones. I could be in Calcutta.

It was a curious sensation, as if I wasn't there. I don't mean the dark faces—there were plenty of them back in Peckham—but I felt exposed and out of place. In a foreign country. I've travelled all over, of course, in my job; compared to lots of people I'm cosmopolitan. But it's different when you're working—you're visiting a place, you're on an outing like the passengers, it's an episode and after a few days you'll be home.

I didn't have a home to go to. I felt raw—I'd

68

felt raw for weeks now, as if my skin had been stripped off. Though it was an obstruction, I felt grateful for the warmth of my enormous coach. I had only driven this one a few times before, in fact Bernie had stuck his *Thank You For Not Smoking* sticker on the windscreen because he drove it the most, but by now it already felt like home. And I'd only been in it a day. But I knew Costas wanted me out of his flat—he had some business contact he owed a favour to, and he wanted to rent it to him. Anyway, it had never felt like mine. I couldn't even remember what its three rooms looked like.

Then I thought about Salim's moustache. It had disturbed me. Were children growing up earlier nowadays? I wondered about my son; would he be more of a man than I had expected? I had presumed to find a little boy like myself. Eleven seemed a bit young for a moustache but it was common knowledge that childhood was shrinking. People put it down to the availability of blue videos and the threat of nuclear war. When I was eleven I'd had nothing on my mind. Children shouldn't be troubled, should they? There was enough of that when they grew up.

Besides, the older he was the more I would have missed. I'd missed such a lot already. I thought of Butler's languor, not to mention his language, and Salim's facial hair; had I lost not only my son's babyhood but his boyhood too? I had a stab of jealousy; the dungaree-ed and undeserving Lesley had had all that and she probably complained too. Perhaps she was telling Edward that just because he knew the Test Match results he was hopelessly *male*.

The foam man drove away in his van. I shifted into gear. Round the corner I found the Sheltered Housing—a modern building in a quiet and luckily wide street. There was room for my coach right outside the door. I drew up, my air brakes sighing.

CHAPTER EIGHT

Mrs Selwyn was sitting in her room watching the boxing on TV.

'Come in,' she called, so I came in.

She was very old, and seemed pleased to see me. This was a relief. All day I had felt like an intruder in other people's lives—a dentist, an Indian, even the market, where I had blocked the vans. But old people welcomed visitors, didn't they? She reminded me of my mother in her last years, when she had been at High Dean, surrounded by photos of me and my Dad, the electric fire on all day. She used to give me her strange rock cakes and tell me I was a blessing. Mrs Selwyn made me some tea, very slowly. It was nice to be offered something for a change. My spirits rose—not because she could help me but simply because I was warm.

'I just happened to be passing,' I said, 'and I was trying to trace some old friends who lived in your street.'

While she boiled the kettle I looked around the room. There were photos along the shelves, and a flowery armchair with that napkin thing on the back to stop your hair getting it greasy. In front of the fire lay an overfed cat. It was like stepping back into my past. She had the *Radio Times* and knitting on the table; I bet she had grandchildren. Outside there was a communal lawn, darkening in the dusk. Odds on she'd never committed adultery with a man in a leather jacket.

'It's nice to see someone young,' she said. I liked that. She gave me a digestive biscuit. 'Someone without any bloody aches and pains.'

'My back plays up sometimes.'

'They're off tonight to the Community Centre,' she said. 'Some bloody sing-song. At least I've kept my wits.'

I sipped my tea and refrained from smoking. My mother had always worried for my lungs; I felt I should behave. I stroked the cat and said: 'I wonder if you knew somebody called Lesley who lived next door to you?'

'Next door?'

'In Talbot Close. She had a little boy called Edward.'

'You mean Eddie?'

I paused, the biscuit halfway to my mouth. I put it down.

'Did I know Eddie?' she chuckled. 'I bloody brought him up.'

The clock chimed. I jumped. It was a heavy mahogany thing; it showed 5.30.

I said: 'You what?'

'Now don't get me wrong,' she said. 'He was a charmer, a real pet. He had a funny little mind.'

She dipped her biscuit into her tea and sucked it. 'He called me Nan.'

'Nan?'

'Thought I was his granny. They don't know any better then, do they?' She picked up her teaspoon and fished the rest of the biscuit out of her cup. 'He had a nap in the afternoon. Once he said he'd seen this story, it had been blown up through his stomach into his head.'

'What?'

'He was dreaming, see. Wasn't that a funny way to put it? Then one day, when he'd had his sleep, he said a man was coming and he was going to take him away in a lorry.'

'What man?'

'Didn't have a Dad, not that I saw. Didn't like to ask. Men are so irresponsible nowadays, aren't they.'

'Are they?'

'You got a smoke?'

Surprised, I fumbled for my cigarettes and

72

gave her one. The cat shifted off my knee. I lit one for myself too.

'What do you mean, you brought him up?' I asked.

'She a friend of yours?'

'Lesley?' I paused. 'Not really.' I always seemed to be saying that.

'Mind you I don't blame her. There was several of them there, you can't tell, can you? She came in one day and started talking about women's lib and I wanted to get down to Ladbroke's because there was a race coming in and I hadn't got the phone then. But there was no stopping her, was there?'

'No,' I said, with feeling.

'And then there she was, gadding off to her ban the bomb meetings and leaving her baby with me because I was an old woman and didn't have nothing else to do.' She sucked at her cigarette. The room had grown darker. 'They all think that. Think they're doing you a favour. I'm quite happy, thank you.'

I felt uneasy, I don't know why. I thought of my mother calling my visits a blessing. Afterwards I'd felt smug, like you feel when you pull in the car to let an ambulance pass—a deeper feeling, of course, but that sort of thing. Had I just felt I was doing my duty?

I stubbed out my cigarette in the ashtray; it hissed.

'I'll tell you something for nothing, young man,' she said. 'She wouldn't have asked my

73

husband.'

'Asked him what?'

'To look after the baby. That's women's blooming lib for you.' She coughed, and passed me her cigarette to put out. It sizzled, and lay next to mine in the puddle of the ashtray.

'Dark so quick,' she said, looking out of the window. 'Sometimes I think I'll just stay in me nightie.'

'Don't say that!' I said. 'Surely there's lots of things to do, there's—'

'God, don't you start.'

The clock chimed again. Another quarter-hour had passed. When I thought about Edward I lost all track of time.

I had a vision of my mother—always, when I arrived, she was in the same chair as I'd left her days before. She always said it was very pleasant and they were very nice. *There's lots of things to do*, she said. Today I remembered the smell of the place—sweetish. The ether that old fruit gives off. It had stayed in my nostrils.

I heard someone shuffling past in the corridor; clunk, clunk, went a walking frame. 'Much good he would have been anyway,' said Mrs Selwyn.

'What?'

'Harold. All the best ones had been taken, see, when I was a girl.'

'Been taken where?'

74

The cat had climbed onto her knee now; she stroked it. 'Taken in France. In their prime.' She glared at me, suddenly irritable. 'The War!' She paused. 'He wasn't up to much.'

'But . . .'

'Got more fun from that little boy, to be honest. He used to belch at dinner.'

'They do, don't they,' I said. 'At that age.'

'Harry,' she said. 'My husband. Aren't you listening?' She glared at me, and went on. 'He used to belch at meals, but only when I was there. Not in company.'

Suddenly I cried out: 'Say you were happy!'

There was a pause. She looked at me, frowning. It was so dark I could hardly see her now. 'They sent you from the Department?' she demanded.

I shook my head.

'You look at my sheets,' she said. 'Nothing wrong with them. Not like some people I could mention.'

I felt helpless. 'What happened to little Eddie?' It felt foreign, calling him that. By now he had become another child; I had so many new things to recollect about him. I needed to go away and think about them.

'You're going to go and say he was neglected,' she said. 'You're chasing him up.' Her voice rose. 'You're going to have him put away!'

I jumped to my feet and stood over her. I bellowed: 'I'm his bloody father!'

There was a silence. Someone shuffled along the corridor outside. The cat jumped off her lap and disappeared.

Then she said: 'You've taken your time.'

'I haven't!' I cried. 'It's not my fault! Tell me where he's gone.'

'Windermere.'

'What?'

'That's where they went, because he sent me a card. Well, she wrote it, of course, but he did the ending.'

She climbed to her feet, went to the cupboard and fished in a drawer.

'Didn't mean to shout,' I mumbled.

She took out a postcard and gave it to me. 'You can keep it,' she said.

I switched on the lamp and looked at the card. One side had a mountain view. The other side read: *Dear Nan, We are living in a lovely room with a view of the lake. It is very nice here, and I can visit the shop downstairs and buy lots of sweeties.* That was Lesley's writing. It was signed with a squiggle. The postmark was six years earlier.

'Can I really keep it?' I asked.

She sighed, then she said: 'I never had any children.'

I replied: 'Well, I haven't really, either.'

*   *   *

In the hallway there was a phone. It was only

just six, so I rang the depot, reversing the charges.

Reg said: 'Where the hell have you been?'

'I've eloped with a coach.'

'I don't give a fuck what she does—'

'A coach,' I said. 'Your coach.'

A pause. 'Where the hell are you?'

'It doesn't matter,' I said.

'What's that supposed to mean? Eight sharp you're booked for Ramsgate.'

I said: 'Get somebody else.'

Reg let rip. I felt strangely detached. Serene, in fact. If this was falling to pieces then it was quite pleasant.

I interrupted him: 'I've worked for you for seven bloody years and I'm having a few days off.'

'I want that fucking coach back by eight tomorrow!'

What had he meant, *a man was going to take him away in a lorry*? Was he dreaming about me? Did he want me to come and take him away? How could Lesley steal my son and then give him to an old lady to look after—what was the point?

It seemed so unfair. Reg's voice buzzed like a mosquito in the earpiece. I thought about my mother in her overheated room; I thought about both my parents, when they were alive, and how they were slipping away from me. I'd presumed all these years that I had remembered them, but it was all becoming confused. Rage rose up in me. I didn't even have any photos. Eleni had chopped them up and the dustmen had been. No human being should do that to another.

That did it—Eleni and her scissors. Reg was yelling about calling the police, so I said, quite calmly: 'If you call the police, I'll tell Joy.'

There was a pause. He said: 'Come again?'

I said: 'If you try to find me I'll phone your wife and tell her that for the past five years you've been knocking off Sonia.'

I had never spoken like this before. It wasn't my style. It was more Eleni's line.

I got into my stride. 'Four gorgeous kids you've got, you big fat randy sod. You don't deserve their—their little toes!' In the hallway, a woman passed in a sequined jacket. She gave me a brilliant smile, like a teenager, and hobbled out of the front door. I shouted down the phone: 'I'll tell your wife about Bournemouth and Cliftonville. I'll tell her about the Isle of Wight.' My voice rose. 'I'll tell her about Sandwich! Dunkirk!' I paused, panting. Then I said: 'I'll tell her about Copenhagen!'

That did it. There was a silence. I replaced the receiver.

*   *   *

I felt tired. It had been a long day. Outside it was dark. Nothing was as it seemed. Reg's

78

wife, I hoped, would never realize this; I wouldn't wish it on anybody. Overnight your house could be blown down and you were out in the cold, shivering. It was so unjust. What had Reg done to deserve the raven-haired and adoring Sonia? What had I done to deserve nothing? There was no sense in it.

What could I trust? Even Mrs Selwyn—she had looked such a grandmother; she should have been one. But cats and fires are deceptive. To tell the truth, she'd shocked me. She'd had no grandchild but my own son, and that reluctantly. She hadn't loved her husband. She had lived with him for years, and yet she thought he wasn't up to much. Who could you rely on nowadays?

I needed a drink. I left the building and walked down the front path. Beside me, the handrail glinted in the light. I wasn't exactly depressed; I was unsettled. In some way, though my limbs ached I felt more alive than I had felt for years. Shouting at Reg had invigorated me. The branches of the trees looked strong and soaring.

I was a few yards from the coach when I realized that something was wrong. For one thing, the door was open. There was something else changed about it too, but it took me a moment to take it in. I'd had so many shocks, and it was still Monday.

I leaped up the steps, into the coach. I stared down the aisle. Rows of faces gazed up

79

at me. There was a pause.

I couldn't see them too clearly in the gloom; they were mostly ladies and they looked settled in their seats, as if they had been there for months.

'We had to get in all by ourselves,' said one of them. 'I don't like to complain.'

Another voice said: 'I'd like to be able to see my knitting.'

I switched on the light. Had I got onto the wrong coach? I swung round, but there were my two cassettes; glued to the side window were Bernie's stickers for the *Austrian Tyrol* and the one saying *We've Been To The Shire Horse Centre*. There was his no smoking sign.

I looked down the aisle. They had come from the Sheltered Housing; they looked tidy and expectant. The sequined lady was there.

'I think you've got on the wrong coach,' I said.

'It is a long coach,' said the sequined lady. 'But it's clean.'

I looked around for help but the street was empty. All day I had been getting in people's way; now, just when I needed them, there was nobody in sight.

'She's such a bossy-boots,' said another voice. 'I don't know why I go.'

'It makes a change,' said another one.

I asked the nearest woman: 'Where are you going?'

She chortled. 'He asks, where are we

going?'

An old man next to her said: 'Can't you see, he's new? He's not the one we had last week.' He addressed me clearly, as if I didn't know English. 'Take us to the Community Centre, sir!'

There was a silence. I was just about to speak, then headlights swung around the far end of the street and I was saved. A moment later another coach pulled in behind me, and the slow business of extricating the old people began.

I helped them down the steps; they thanked me warmly. One wore a hairnet with little diamonds in it; as she nodded, they winked. Everyone was polite. Now they were leaving the coach it looked bigger than before, and emptier. I've noticed that before, when passengers have disembarked. All those dark, tartan seats.

A sing-song sounded cheerful; besides, I didn't have any other plans for that evening. I imagined us linking arms. I've noticed in my job: it's only the very old, and the very young, who can sing without getting pissed first.

I gripped one frail arm after another, helping them down. I thought: what about Windermere? Would I really go there? I couldn't imagine any possible way of finding my son.

The last woman paused in the street and fumbled in her handbag. 'I'm Winifred,' she said. 'I'd like you to know, this is not what I'm accustomed to.'

'I'm sorry,' I said. 'Sorry about the muddle.'

'I don't mean that.' She pointed to the people climbing into the other coach. 'I mean, to them.'

She wore a fur-trimmed coat. There was a brooch pinned to her chest; it was a brass tree, upside down. She smiled, and pressed something into my hand. It was 10p.

CHAPTER NINE

I drove out of Leicester through the rush hour traffic. It always takes me by surprise, that other towns have rush hours. Where were they going? Streams of cars and buses were hurtling into the blackness. Where did everybody live? It unnerved me, to think of the number of people out there, in thousands of places I would never see. Did they know the secret of how to bring up a family? I'd read the divorce statistics, of course, and TV nowadays was full of weeping women—why is it only the women who weep?—but I still felt that the heart of England was doors closed on contentment. Car in the garage; everything safe. I'd once had a toy farmyard and I'd found it satisfying, to put the tractor into the barn and then, the next morning, to take it out again.

I was driving north. I had made up my mind to go to Windermere. I was having a holiday, after all, and people went to Windermere for their holidays. Perhaps not in November, but still. Before I left the town I pulled up at a late-night shop and bought myself razors, toothpaste and a toothbrush. That fixed it; with my plastic bag I was now officially adrift. It was like going through an airport Departure Lounge; there was no turning back.

I had been to the Lake District before; I'd driven a couple of Lakeland Heritage Tours. Besides, I had been there on holiday when I was fifteen; already I had something in common with my son. My parents and I had stayed in a village Bed and Breakfast; we had gone on hikes over the fells, with frequent stops to peruse the map, and my father had worn his shorts which I was old enough to find embarrassing. Governments had crumbled, rain forests had fallen, President Reagan ruled the world and so did AIDS, but you could still rely on one thing, and that was the good old mountains.

I had no idea how to find Lesley and Edward. The only clue I had was a flat that overlooked the lake, and was above a sweet-shop. The poor little blighter probably hadn't got any teeth left.

But at least I would be there. Tomorrow, I would be in a place that was familiar to my son. I might glimpse him in the street; I might

83

find them in the phone-book. I felt like a hunter tracking his prey and finding one camping-place after another, with its cold ash and empty tins. Each time I spotted a clue there was a bump of recognition. I was living his life, years later; I was treading in his childish footprints. Already I knew his first and second streets; I had spoken to a boy who had played with him and an old lady who had listened to his dreams. And I was getting nearer. I had already covered five years. It was just a matter of time, surely, until I came across a campfire and found its ashes were still warm.

*   *   *

I left Leicester behind. It had become oddly familiar. I presumed this was because my son had lived there, but actually it was the people I'd met who stuck in my mind: the beautiful, bashful Indian wife—how unlike any woman I'd ever known—the elderly Mrs Selwyn, even the woman in the maroon coat who had grabbed me for a moment in belligerent intimacy. It was so daft. A few minutes' exertions on Lesley's mattress and eleven years later I was stuck in a Leicester cul-de-sac being called a pervert. I thought of Winifred, the last lady to get off the coach, and I knew there was something vital about her brooch. But I was too tired to work out what it was.

The traffic had disappeared, to wherever it is that traffic goes. I was in the countryside now, driving towards Derby. It was so chilly that my breath smoked; I turned up the heater. Signs loomed out of the dark. I pictured a pint of bitter and a plate of shepherd's pie. Mealtimes had begun to be important.

After twenty minutes I saw a pub ahead. It was strung with fairy lights. Slowing down, I saw that it was charmingly olde worlde, a Free House with rosy light through the curtains. When I was young I thought Free House meant you didn't have to pay—how my Dad had chuckled; he was a chartered accountant.

But then I saw the sign. NO COACHES. I swerved back on to the road and drove on. This annoyed me. According to Lesley the world discriminated against women. What about coach drivers dying for a pee? I changed into second and steamed up a hill. What about ordinary blokes in anoraks who happened to be standing at school gates? Come to think of it, I'd had some funny looks in playgrounds too. Once when I'd asked a woman the age of her son she had moved to the next bench.

I found a motel near Derby and stopped for the night. It was a depressing place with muzak in the toilets. I was so tired that I nodded off over my gammon steak. Afterwards I tried to exorcise Eleni by having an Irish Coffee. It was her favourite tipple; if I drank it enough times it would no longer remind me of her.

The bar was empty except for a foursome in the adjoining cubicle. The women were talking about postnatal exercises. One of them said: 'Connie tightens her pelvic muscles when she's watching TV. She does it when the ads come on.'

At this point one of the men cleared his throat and asked the other: 'So how does it feel, Dennis, to be driving the Car of the Year?'

* * *

I gave up on the Irish Coffees and switched to scotch. I looked at my watch: it was 9.15. When you've lost your wife something happens to time. It's almost normal in the daylight hours, but once you get to the evening it stops. Well, it inches forward, but it never gets anywhere. Whenever you look at your watch there's a whole evening ahead.

I gave in at 9.45 and went to bed. I looked at myself in the mirror: five foot nine, sandy hair—receding, a bit. Boyishness gone, for good. I'd hung on for years.

I had nothing to read except a local paper I'd found jamming the wardrobe door shut, so I gazed at tenders for farm machinery and fell asleep.

* * *

I dreamed I was sitting astride a roof. The sun was shining and the slates were hot; they scorched my groin. The next house along had an attic window and somebody was rattling its frame. I couldn't see who it was but I knew it was urgent and I had to get to them. I worried that the window was loose and knew I should have fixed it but all my tools were packed up in a Transit van down in the street. I inched along the ridge of the roof; it took a long time, I was starting to panic and a burning sensation spread down my thighs and up my stomach. But however hard I tried I didn't get any nearer, and for some reason I didn't want to, I wanted to stay on my roof, and soon I realized that the rattling had stopped. Whoever it was had given up.

When I woke it was three in the morning and I'd had my first wet dream for years.

*   *   *

I told you I was superstitious. When I woke next the sun was shining and the sky was that solid blue that makes your eyeballs ache. What a terrific omen! I headed across country towards the M6.

When I got to Windermere I planned to buy some underpants and a pair of pyjamas. It was the sort of old-fashioned town that would still have a gents' outfitters. Eleni hadn't let me wear pyjamas—she had giggled at mine and

87

said I looked like a dirty old man—but they made me feel secure and there was no Eleni now, giggling and sneering and cheating at Scrabble.

It wasn't her cheating, actually, that was annoying. It was the way she wrong-footed me. Suddenly she would want to play a game—she wore that bright, hectic look that made me wary—and then halfway through, just when I'd found a good word like 'EPISTLE', she'd get bored. Worse than that—contemptuous. 'What a stupid game,' she'd sigh, and for her next word she'd lay out 'SO'. She wasn't great at Scrabble but she was better than that. What can you do with women? They play games with you all the time, and when the moment comes to play a real one they suddenly cop out and make you foolish.

A son would understand. I had high hopes of Edward this morning. Not only was he 'absolutely gorgeous' (Pam) and 'a charmer' (Mrs Selwyn): he was a chap.

*   *   *

Beyond Stoke-on-Trent I joined the M6. Travelling along the middle lane, I wondered why Lesley had gone to Windermere. It was the sort of place where people retired and I wondered if her parents lived there. I knew so little about her. If I knew their town I could have phoned them, the grandparents of my child, and saved myself a lot of bother.

I felt resentful, that she hadn't got on with them; it was so thoughtless of her. This made us suddenly close, as if she had been sitting beside me in the coach, biting her nails. Love makes a woman vague, doesn't it? She appears all misty. Irritation, on the other hand, pulls her close, crystal-clear. My mother said that after Dad died she missed him the most when she found the things that had always annoyed her, like his cigarette burns on the loo windowsill.

I slotted in The Shadows for the third time. Perhaps Lesley hadn't joined her parents; perhaps she had become a spinsterly Lake District person, wearing a jerkin and driving a Metro. There were lots of women like that there, middle-aged before their time. Perhaps she had become a social worker. Perhaps she had opted out and lived in a farmhouse, ruddy-faced and breeding sheep. Edward would stomp about in the mud and shoot crows with his catapult. They would welcome me with a mug of tea and I would fix the guttering, a man at last.

It was such a beautiful morning. An hour passed. I drove through the industrial areas—Warrington, signs to Wigan—and speeded North. The countryside changed; it was emptier now, with more sky on top. Perhaps she had become a well-known sociologist; she went to Lancaster University and lectured about the changing patterns of family life in the '80s. She knew all the statistics but what was she telling her own son? When he put up his hand to ask about his own family pattern did her fluency desert her?

I wasn't going to feel bitter. That wouldn't do us any good. Who wants a large strange man on the doorstep haranguing your mother? This was one of the things I had decided. I hadn't decided much else, actually. I had never been much of a planner—if I had, I'd have had a better job by now; I'd be running my own business and using my brains. I hadn't planned what I was going to do when I met them—reveal my identity at once or pretend I'd come to read the meter? I hadn't planned what I'd do if she was married with two children and a socking great husband blocking the doorway. For some reason I couldn't picture this. She wasn't the marrying type; I had convinced myself. If you'd known Lesley, you would understand.

Another hour had passed. It was 12.30. The countryside was showing its bones now; rocks jutted from fields. It was bleak and bare and after Lancaster the motorway was emptier. I was getting near.

I sang out loud that Frank Ifield number *I remember you*—actually I didn't like it much but I could do the yodelling bit, *You-hoo*. Edward would admire that; not many men can yodel. I could teach him how to do it, and my four different whistles. It was a shame for them to die out.

*   *   *

KENDAL AND THE LAKES. I indicated left and turned off the motorway. Ahead, I caught my first glimpse of the mountains. They were piled up in the distance like stormclouds—rosy pink and purple. They were breathtaking. I thought of Edward growing up amongst such beauty and felt an unfamiliar sensation towards Lesley: gratitude. *I remember too, distant bells . . .*

As I neared Windermere I slowed down. Now I was close I wanted to delay it; I'd felt this way in Leicester. Driving along the motorway was easy, my head whirled with possibilities. Now I felt nervous. I crawled along at 30 mph. The road twisted between drystone walls; behind them, sheep bleated. A Landrover flashed its lights and overtook me; it was spattered with mud. Even in the coach I could breathe the sharp new air.

What was I going to do with him? Take him out for a hamburger and then drive back to London? Move nearby and become part of his life? My palms were sticky. I felt I was going on a first date.

I turned off the road and drove into Windermere. The high street was narrow; I barely scraped past the parked cars. On each

91

side were houses with *Bed and Breakfast* signs, all with *Vacancies.*

Without warning, my spirits slumped. I was stupid to think that anybody would stay here long; it was a tourist town, millions of people passed through it each year, munching Kendal Mint Cake and scattering litter. Lesley and Edward wouldn't be here, and after all this time who would remember them?

I parked in a coach park I had used years before—at least this place had facilities—and climbed down. My back ached; I had been driving for hours. I walked up the road, into the shopping street. On a November Tuesday there weren't many people about. A couple of teenagers passed, wearing climbing boots; a woman loaded groceries into her car. There were three sweet-shops, selling postcards and souvenirs, but none of them overlooked the lake. In fact, I remembered now, the lake was a mile away. I shivered. Not only did I need pyjamas; I needed some gloves. I found a gents' outfitters but it was so old-fashioned it had closed down.

I decided to walk the mile to the lake. There were more shops there, I remembered them—souvenir shops and a hotel, where I had once taken a tour for tea. I started down the main road. As I passed the bungalows, with their rockeries and *Vacancies* signs, I suddenly thought: I'm only doing this so I don't have to go back to London.

I shut myself up. What a way to carry on. My son had probably biked along this road a hundred times. When school finished I might glimpse him free-wheeling round the corner, fresh-faced and whistling. I'd call his name: 'Edward! Eddie!' He would jam on his brakes and wobble to a halt.

I felt numb. I tried to make this place come alive. I tried to remember my holiday, when I was fifteen. Was it Windermere we had visited, or was it Ambleside? We'd sat in some teashop somewhere. I couldn't remember; my brain had locked.

When I got down to the Lake it was no good. Most of the shops sold souvenirs and were closed for the winter; their view of the lake seemed to be blocked by the Old England Hotel, and now I had got there I couldn't be bothered to investigate further.

This alarmed me. I felt vaguely ill and sat on a bench overlooking the lake. The sun had gone in and the water was steely; a gust of wind blew, shivering it. I had forgotten about lunch. This made me panic-stricken, I usually remember food. I should be hungry. I should be having a bite and then briskly conducting my enquiries. What was the matter?

I looked down at my hands; they seemed a long way away, as they had seemed when I'd sat in the kitchen and the room had begun to echo. They didn't belong to me; they looked bleached and freckly. My arms looked inert. I heard sinister, small lapping sounds, the waves on the beach, and I heard Eleni's voice, far off, saying she'd had enough of me. *Enough,* she lapped, *enough.* Without her face to distract me, I noticed for the first time the whiney quality of her voice. Above me the kitchen stretched higher. I asked myself: what did I do wrong? I heard the faint sounds of traffic, and the lapping water. If I could remember the day of the week, then I wouldn't be going mad.

Why had I landed up here? Of course I didn't have a son. Just for the moment, I couldn't even remember his name. What was it? Why one name rather than another? My name is Desmond Stephen Fletcher. I've never felt like a Desmond, not really; that was the trouble, I've felt more like a Bruce. My mother hadn't got me right. *Bruce,* the water laps. It would be a hoot to have a new name. I couldn't be expecting to find my son because I hadn't bothered to comb my hair.

It seems like weeks since I've opened my mouth and talked to anybody; my throat feels dry. I'm propped up, inside my empty skin. Perhaps; if Bruce had been me, he'd be having a nervous breakdown too. I want to be tucked up under my duvet, but it isn't my duvet anymore, it has a blue pattern on it. Had I really come here on holiday? I can't remember being fifteen, it's too long ago. To tell the truth, I think I was bored. We sat in bloody teashops all the time. I can't remember my mother's face, and if I try to concentrate I feel sick. I must try to remember the name of the estate agents in Orpington. *No home today*, the waves lap. I realize, with mild curiosity, that I'm shaking.

*   *   *

No home today. Somebody was speaking: *No home today.*

'You okay?'

A man was standing in front of me. I lifted my head from my knees.

'You okay?' he repeated. He was eating a sausage roll.

'Fine.'

I got to my feet. Then I walked back up the hill and checked into the first Bed and Breakfast I found. It was a chilly room but it had a bed. I took off my anorak, trousers and shoes, climbed in between the sheets and slept for fifteen hours.

CHAPTER TEN

I suddenly woke up and saw Winifred's brooch. Of course, now I knew why it was so familiar. I blessed her for being so old she had pinned the tree upside down.

It was dark. Through the wall I could hear a

baby crying; it went on and on, as if somebody was sawing logs. It took me a while to realize where I was. I pinched my watch; it was 5 am.

The brooch looked like a CND badge. Lesley had always worn one on her army coat; I remembered teasing her about her anti-military stance when there she was, togged up like a sergeant-major. She had never appreciated my jokes.

I lay back in bed. I felt airy and wide-awake. Her fear of nuclear attack was her strongest emotion; in fact I had worried about Edward growing up with such despair. Wherever she lived, she would join the CND. All I had to do was to phone up the local branch and get her address.

I jumped out of bed and opened the door. The light dazzled me. I blinked, and tried to focus. A girl was standing in the corridor, rocking a baby. I pulled down my shirt-front.

'Is there a phone?' I asked.

She didn't reply. Her face was pimply; she was very young.

I repeated it. 'Is there a phone?'

She gazed back at me. Was she the daughter of the house? I hadn't seen her the day before. The baby started crying again and she heaved it over her shoulder, like luggage, and went into the next bedroom. Through the nightie I could see her narrow buttocks. She closed the door.

Then I realized it was only five in the

morning, so I went back to bed.

*　　　*　　　*

The nearest CND office was in Kendal, ten miles away. I phoned several times but there was no reply. My landlady, a silent, stocky woman, stood behind me in the hall, polishing her pictures with Windolene. They were framed prints of British birds; I heard the puff-puff of her aerosol. I felt better this morning; what had happened to me yesterday? It seemed a week ago. I must have had what my mother would call a turn. What a twit I was, to feel it was all hopeless.

At 10.15 a man answered. He sounded friendly, but then he had a Scottish accent. I asked him if he could give me the address of somebody called Lesley Featherstone; who was, perhaps still, a member of CND and lived, perhaps still lived, in Windermere.

'Sorry, mate,' he said. 'We don't give out the addresses of our members.'

*　　　*　　　*

Half an hour later I was in Kendal, parking near the cattle market. I had no plan of attack; I just wanted to be busy. For a moment, in fact, I had forgotten all about my son. This was a challenge, like finding a missing electrical connection when you're mending the stereo.

97

Wholesome women in tweed coats strode by; everybody wore headscarves. The air cut my London lungs. I had to remind myself it was Wednesday; after my deep sleep I felt dislocated. A sweet-shop window was piled with fireworks and I realized it was still October 31; I had even got the month wrong.

I walked up a flight of stone steps to a first floor office. The door was open. It was a cluttered room. There was nobody there except for a middle-aged woman with her arms full of flowers. I stopped in the doorway.

'I'm not really here!' she cried.

I stared at her. Perhaps she wasn't. After all, I had never seen that girl in the nightie again. Sunlight slanted through the window onto her chrysanthemums.

'This the CND?' I asked.

She nodded; so did her flowers. She had a strong, leathery face and wore a Sherlock Holmes hat. 'I'm supposed to be doing the flowers in church,' she said. 'It's such a curse.'

'What is?'

'My son asked me to hold the fort.' Behind her hung a poster of a mushroom cloud; it seemed to be rising from her head. 'He's taking his daughter to playgroup. Why his wife can't do it, quite honestly, is beyond me.'

I paused. 'I'm a mate of his,' I said. 'Leave it to me.'

She frowned. 'Are you sure?'

*   *   *

I listened to her footsteps going down the stairs. The next moment I was fumbling through a drawerful of index cards. Some were yellowed; I hoped they weren't out of date. *Forster . . . Fairlie . . . Flexner . . . Faversham.* I couldn't work out the alphabet; I must be going to bits.

But then I realized that somebody else had mis-filed them. For some reason it was a relief, feeling I was less scatty than another person. I was sweating. At any moment the Scots bloke would be coming back. I flicked through the cards; my fingertips felt sore.

Just as I found Lesley, I heard his footsteps on the stairs. *Lesley Featherstone, 38 Laurel Road.* I memorized it, pushed back the drawer of the filing cabinet and pressed myself against it.

He came in. He was a slight chap, wearing a lumberjack's shirt.

'Can I help you?' he asked.

I steadied my breath. Then I said: 'I was wondering if I could apply for membership.'

*   *   *

I wore my badge on my anorak. I'd nothing against the CND; besides, it might soften Lesley up.

My stomach churned. I walked down

99

towards the cattle market. The sight of her typed address had transformed this town, as if I was seeing it through another camera lens. My legs felt springy.

I went into a W H Smith and found a *Beezer*, *Beano* and *Mad*. When I lifted them from the rack, my hand was trembling. I felt different today; I realized that I hadn't truly believed I'd find him in London or Leicester. He was so close now; he was breathing behind me. I looked at a *Daily Mail*. Above a photo of Princess Di was a headline about the American hostages, still being held in Beirut. My son, too, was waiting to be rescued. Innocent, he didn't even know the footsteps were getting nearer.

'George, old cock!' One man slapped another on the back. They were friendly, up here, in the shops. Today, ruddy and expansive, everybody was on my side. They knew the value of family life; women didn't commit adultery, they devoted themselves to flower arrangements.

I went over to the cassettes. I had never noticed how many were made for children. I inspected the display of Favourite Fairy Stories, read aloud by TV personalities. He was too old for *Puss in Boots*, I decided. *Sinbad the Sailor* was more his line. An assistant was stocking some shelves nearby; he was no more than a boy himself.

'What would you recommend, chief?' I

100

asked him. 'For a bloke of eleven?' I paused. 'My son.'

'There's Madonna,' he said, pointing. 'Duran Duran.'

'Not pop music!' I cried. 'He's a child!'

The assistant shrugged. I turned back and selected *Sinbad* and *The Wind in the Willows*. My parents had taken me to the panto and I had laughed at Mr Toad.

*　　*　　*

I was back in Windermere by 11.30. It was another sunny day; the mountains were pasteboardy, like a stage set, and near enough to touch. I drove down to the lakeside and parked outside the Old England. My coach blocked the entrance, but they would presume I'd decanted some old biddies for elevenses. The lake was bright blue, like a swimming pool; it didn't seem real. It was a different lake today. I was humming, to calm my nerves. I tried to remember the words of *Eleanor Rigby*; that usually did the trick.

I combed my hair, left Edward's comics in the coach and locked it up. Behind the first row of shops I found Laurel Road. It curved away from me; it was possible that some of the top-floor windows had a view of the lake. Why had I been so spineless yesterday? A woman passed, pulling along a bull terrier; it looked like Frankie Howerd. She said 'Good morning' to me as if I had a right to be there.

I passed a knitting shop (14), a baker's (16) and a chemist's (18). Which of his childhood illnesses had I missed: chicken pox, measles? Did he have asthma? I glanced inside the shop; it was reassuring, the way everyone here was middle-aged.

I turned the corner. There was nothing.

I stopped and stared. The last building this side of the road, number 20, had been sliced like cake and sealed with plastic. From then on it was open space. To be exact: car park. A large, gravelled, empty car park surrounded by newly-planted shrubs.

I leant against a shop window. My face felt hot and swollen. I had driven three hundred miles to look at a patch of gravel.

I went into the shop. It was a butcher's. A man with a mottled face, wearing a boater, said: 'And good morning to you.' Behind him hung a pig, with its stomach split open.

My tongue felt thick. I pointed: 'What happened to there?'

'Where?'

'They shouldn't have done that.'

'Something's up?' He moved from behind the counter. I stopped him. 'No,' I said. 'I mean, why did they build a car park?'

'You ask why?' He gazed at me. Behind him the pig, suspended by its hind legs, stared at the floor. Its mouth was open. 'You seen this place in season? You seen the trippers? Seen

102

the charabancs?' He pointed out of the window. 'So they go and build that for the coaches. And let me tell you something: now it's like blooming Oxford Street. My customers, these whoppers come along and they have to stand against the wall like it's a firing squad. I ask them: any last requests?' He guffawed. There was a brown smear on his apron. The pig, snout-down, gazed noiselessly at the floor.

I said: 'Do you remember a sweet-shop?'

He nodded. 'Fudge and stuff. Had to move away, didn't they. To Spain.'

'They've moved away?'

He nodded again. 'Well, he was Armenian.'

'Armenian?'

'Something like that.'

I paused. 'So they've gone?' This wasn't my lucky day. I tried once more. 'Do you remember a woman who lived above it, with a little boy?'

He thought for a moment, wiping his big red hands on his apron. 'In a wheelchair?'

'No, a pushchair.' Then I realized Edward would be too old for that.

He shook his head. 'Wheelchair. He was disabled.'

There was a silence; I don't know for how long.

Then I whispered: 'What do you mean, disabled?'

'He was all right in the head,' said the

103

butcher. 'It was the rest of him. I carried him up the stairs once; he was as light as a feather.'

I couldn't speak. My throat had closed. The door squeaked behind me; a customer had come in. I asked: 'What was his name?'

'Light as a feather. Couldn't believe he was fourteen.'

He asked the customer what she wanted and she said two chump chops. I said: 'Fourteen?'

He lifted a knife and started slicing. 'His Mum had an account. That's right—Terence. His name was Terence.'

*　　　*　　　*

I drove out of Windermere. I didn't know where I was going; I had to move my coach, two waiters had been staring at it. I drove out of the town and found myself steaming up a narrow, winding lane with stone walls on either side; they nearly scraped my paintwork. I met a lorry and pulled in. The lorry was crammed with sheep; their grey wool bulged between the slats. They bleated like old women. I wound up the window; they smelt sour.

I was shivering. Should I drive back to London? My throat had narrowed and my eyes prickled. I drove on, up the hill, past a farmyard and a fir wood, past two bungalows with picture windows, past a muddy pony with its head lolling over a gate. I hadn't changed my underwear for three days; this wasn't like me. Nothing made sense any more. Why did they pull down that house? Why did everybody go away? Why did I confuse my son with another? I thought of the butcher lifting the boy, with his frail bones: did he put his arms around the butcher's neck? Had he grown bigger now? *Eat up your mince*, my mother used to say, *and you'll be a nice big boy.* You grew up, but what was the point?

I turned a corner and jolted to a halt. Suddenly I was face to face with the mountains. I had arrived at the top of a hill; the Lake District was spread out in front of me. The peaks were bathed in rosy light; it was the most beautiful view I had ever seen. I turned off the engine; my throat swelled and the mountains blurred. At first I thought I was having an attack of hiccups, but then I realized I was crying.

I didn't have a handkerchief. I snuffled into the windscreen cloth, which smelt of oil. What was the matter with me? I jerked and shuddered. It was a shock, I suppose, hearing about the wheelchair; it could so easily have been my own son.

But really, what was the difference? My son might not be disabled, but another son was. It was just as bad. How could anybody bear a world this cruel? We fed our children mince: for what?

Sitting in my coach that afternoon, I don't

think I was crying for one boy, or even two. I was crying for all of them. And I suppose for me, too.

*   *   *

I felt emptied and sore afterwards, as if I'd vomited. I drove around for a while, looking for a pub, but then I realized it was 4.30. What had happened to the day? I drove back into Windermere and bought myself a hot pasty. A police car cruised past. I wondered if Reg had sent out my particulars, but I knew I was safe. Reg's father-in-law ran the biggest travel agent's in Peckham; Reg wouldn't risk his marriage, let alone his business, for the sake of a coach.

I was getting fond of my Panorama Elite. Outside its doors I felt increasingly exposed; inside it I felt safe. A bloke hanging around a street gets some funny looks, but a bloke sitting in a coach is just a driver. He must be waiting for somebody.

*   *   *

To tell the truth, my mother wasn't much of a cook. I hadn't put it into words until today, when I'd remembered her mince. It wasn't nearly as tasty as the school stuff. Once I'd gone into the kitchen and found her crying. She was mashing potato. It had scared me out of my wits. There was her back view, shaking; the bow of her apron hadn't been tied properly, which alarmed me. She didn't know I was there. I realized now that she had large legs—fat, really.

Then she turned. Her face was contorted; it was the most terrifying thing I had ever seen in my life. She covered her face with her hand, quickly, and said in a level voice: 'Pop out and get some firelighters.' I had tried to reply; I said: 'Honestly, Mum, we don't mind the lumps.' She turned away and said: 'Pop out, Desmond.'

For thirty years I had forgotten about this. At the time I had presumed she was worried about her cooking. You feel secure, don't you, when you give yourself that sort of reason? Children want to feel secure. I thought of the three of us watching *Sunday Night at the London Palladium* on TV; now I remembered the noise that had accompanied it—my father's snores. Fathers slept, mothers cooked. That's what families did, didn't they? That was all I knew.

I had done my best to carry on the family tradition. My mother wasn't like Eleni; she hadn't nudged Dad's ribs and sniggered to her female friends. *He wasn't up to much*, Mrs Selwyn had said. Why had her words filled me with fear?

*   *   *

I started up the coach and drove back towards the M6. But instead of by-passing Kendal I drove in and parked beside the cattle market again. Shops which had just opened this morning were closing up now; it was hard to believe that a day had passed. Since I'd left London the clocks had taken on a life of their own. Today the hours had disappeared down a sort of funnel.

The Scots bloke was in the office. He was trying to open a plastic cup of soup. He looked up and said: 'Why did you say you were a mate of mine?'

'I was lonely.'

He grinned, got the lid off, swore and sucked his fingers.

It was true, actually. I hadn't had a conversation for days. Weeks. Years. I said: 'Did you know Lesley Featherstone?'

'Sure.'

'You did?'

'She was always pinching my fags.' He took a sip of soup and grimaced.

I removed a pile of envelopes from a chair and sat down. 'Did you know her well? Where did she go?'

'She came to the sit-in at Sellafield. Had a great pair of lungs on her.' He took another sip. 'This isn't tomato. We delivered some leaflets together.'

'Why was she here? What was she doing?'

'I think she worked at a pub,' he said.

'Which one?'

'Dunno.' He drained his soup. 'That was minestrone.'

'Why was she here?'

'Because of Barry, I guess.'

I paused. 'What?'

'She lived with him. They had a kid.'

I stared. He put his empty container into an overflowing bin. After a moment I asked: 'Who was he?'

He looked at me. 'She a relative or something?'

'Not really.'

'He worked on the boats at Windermere. Big chap, chest hair. Dunno what he did in the winter.'

'How long were they here?' I asked.

'About a year.'

I paused. Then I asked casually: 'What about the boy? What was he like?'

'Nice kid. Only saw him once or twice.'

'Do you know where they've gone?'

He shook his head. Then he looked at me. 'You okay?' There was a pause, then he said: 'Fancy a drink?'

*　　　*　　　*

Robbie could put them away; so, that evening, could I. We sat in a snug, populated by a few very old men, and drank. I liked him. He had a

109

twinkly look, and a Zapata moustache, and he called his drinking delaying tactics. Like Lesley, he was intelligent. Unlike her, he was a bloke. She was muddy and female; he was as clear as water and cracked some terrific jokes. I can't remember what we talked about; you can never remember the sort of things you say in pubs, can you? It's a different kind of talk; it was just what I wanted. At one point I asked him why women never had a sense of humour. 'Because it's us poor sods who need it,' he replied. I asked him why and he asked me to supper. Then he told me a story about Mrs Thatcher's chauffeur, and another about some Polish geezer at Glasgow University, where he'd been a student, and then a couple of pints later we got on to limericks. He stood up, swaying; the old gents turned their heads.

> *'There was once a young lady from Brighton,*
> *Whose boyfriend said "You've got a tight 'un,"*
> *Said she, "'Pon my soul,*
> *You're up the wrong hole,*
> *There's plenty of room in the right 'un"'*

Soon after that he looked at his watch, shrank somehow, and got to his feet.

We left the pub arm in arm. He hadn't got transport so I offered him a lift. We walked down to the cattle market. There was a line of cars parked there, in the dark. He stopped beside them. I dragged him away and pointed

110

to my coach. It filled the end of the street, glimmering in the glow from a Chinese takeaway. As always, I felt pleased to see it. Tonight, with a few pints inside me, it looked magnificent. It was so big that the street lamp sat on its roof.

He was dead chuffed. It was like having a child with me. He bounced on the seats; I had to show him how the gears worked—not much different from anything else, actually. He sat in the driving seat, playing with the levers. We slotted in Ricky Nelson. Raising my voice over the music I shouted modestly: 'It's not one of your in-flight, executive whatsits, no bar facility or video facility or, ho ho, hostess facility. That's for the big boys. My boss is a small boy.' I measured an inch, between my finger and thumb. 'Very small. Like this.'

It felt odd, like showing somebody around my house for the first time. I realized how many things had accumulated on the floor. Robbie picked up the *Beano*. 'Dennis the Menace!' he cried. 'You regressive old git!'

'It's not for me,' I said. 'It's for my son.'

I had started the engine. He leaned forward. 'Left at the lights,' he said. 'Your son?'

I told him about it: how Edward wasn't Barry's but mine. I think he was a bit pissed, that's why he didn't sound surprised. I was a touch oiled, too, because tonight it seemed the most natural thing in the world, to suddenly want to look for my son. After all, what's a few

111

years, give or take a decade?

He said: 'Take one of mine! I've got plenty to spare.' He chuckled. 'One less nappy to change.'

Alarmed, I said: 'I've never changed a nappy.'

'Come on, say yes. Do me a favour. There's nothing in the world as detumescing,' he intoned, 'as a houseful of kids.'

We drove through the streets of Kendal. It was only 8.30 but the place was deserted; it's like that in country towns. Tall stone buildings, like cliffs, reared up on either side. We passed a mill with its smoking chimney. Streetlamps glowed. I felt we were on the stage of some comic opera from Dickens's time. I wasn't here; by now my journey seemed unreal. I was locked into some epic voyage—that would take me across Britain, all odd views and odd people and blind, unlikely cul-de-sacs.

'Bugger women,' I said.

'Bugger 'em.'

'They're all bitches.'

'Piff's not a bitch.' He sighed. 'Let me tell you something, Desmond, oh sonless one, coach driver extraordinaire, lost soul in this universe of keening men, menopausal malcontent in this long pub-crawl we call life—'

'Get on with it.'

'What was I saying?'

'Bitches.'

112

'Bitches. Yours might've been bitches, but take it from me, it's much, much, much worse when they're nice.' He leant forward and pointed. 'Second on the left. Most women use sledgehammers. Piff, on the other hand, uses the microstrobic—microspitic—minuscule, minute, highly-tuned needle-sharp instruments of a Nobel-prize-winning brain surgeon. Here! Stop.'

I stopped, with a judder, outside a row of cottages. We climbed down. He spent a while searching for his door-keys. The door opened. A gaunt, beautiful girl dressed like a refugee stood amidst the ruins.

'Piff, this is my old mate Desmond,' he shouted. 'Desmond, this is my wife Philippa.' Children's cries drowned his voice. 'He's come to buy one of the kids!'

'Your mother came round,' she said. The ruins she stood amongst were children's toys. A small boy leapt on Robbie, like a monkey, and slid down again. Robbie scooped him up and lifted him above his head.

'Darling,' she said warningly.

'I'm perfectly okay,' he said. 'Look, no hands!'

'I didn't know where you were, so I gave her some coffee. She sat here for hours. I haven't even bathed the children yet. She caught Gavin eating the cat's food.'

'Sorry, sorry,' he said.

'I just wish you'd phone,' she said, 'I'm

113

supposed to finish these drawings for Mike. I know that it's hardly any money, and I'm a bit rusty—'

He turned to me. 'There's a subtext here.'

'What's a subtext?' I asked.

'Darling, you're an angel,' he said to his wife. 'You're all things—wife, mother, hamster-catcher, fridge-defroster, lover, nurse, deeply talented graphic designer. Oh, let me put my hand up your subtexts!' He turned to me. 'Come on. Action stations!'

*   *   *

We fetched two cans of McEwan's and went upstairs with the children. There seemed to be four of them. I carried the little girl, but she said I smelt funny and wriggled out of my arms. I had never bathed a child before; they seemed to have so many clothes, with so many buttons and little strips of Velcro. I knew there was something I had to remember about Barry, but I couldn't think what it was. How could anyone think of anything, with children?

They were as slippery as eels and only one would let me wash him. Another slid on the lino, bumped into the toilet and cried. The smallest boy stood up in the bath, and peed. Jamie, the eldest, ticked me off for smoking and said I would die, like his father. The bathroom was strewn with wet clothes and the children kept running away to watch television.

114

The little girl sat on my knee, despite my breath, and tenderly played with my hand; at least, I thought she was. In fact she was using my fingernail to clean her own fingernails. Robbie was in high spirits; he played hide-and-seek with the bare children, bumping into the furniture. Piff called upstairs: 'Please, darling, don't get them excited!'

*   *   *

Supper was tense. I decided, not for the first time, that if only women drank, life would be easier. Piff sipped at a glass of orange juice. My head ached; the Aga made the room stuffy. They had invited me to spend the night, which was kind because my funds were running low. I could sleep on the sofa. I was trapped; she had put my clothes into the washing machine. I wore a pair of Robbie's underpants and one of his checked shirts.

He was right; she was nice. I liked both of them, but I could hardly breathe. It felt as if we were being wrapped in bandages and someone was pulling them tighter. I had forgotten what marriage was like; in fact, by comparison mine seemed quite simple. They turned to me and told me things I didn't want to know. Piff told me Robbie had had a vasectomy. We finished our scrambled eggs. I started telling them about the time I took a group of nuns to Inverness, then Robbie

115

suddenly said: 'Piff thinks I'm too busy saving the world to care about my family.'

There were short moments of silence. A child came downstairs. Piff told him to go to bed. Robbie hugged him. Piff snapped at Robbie. The child started crying. Piff said: 'Now look what you've done.' My head throbbed. I was sitting on something damp; it was a tomato. Piff turned to me and said: 'Would you believe it, I was once Miss Lovely Legs of Glasgow College of Art.'

The food sobered me up, just a bit, and I wondered what I was going to do. Tomorrow I would have to go back to London. Robbie was not only younger than me, he was smaller; his shirt chafed my armpits. I wondered what it was really like, bringing up children. Was it really like this?

I decided to have one last go. I leaned across to Pitt and asked: 'Did you know Lesley Featherstone?'

'Lesley?'

Robbie said: 'The woman who talked all the time, remember? She was shagging that bloke called Barry.'

'Ah, that Lesley,' she said. 'The one who smashed our car.'

'It was only a dent,' he said.

'Were they hurt?' I cried.

'No.'

I smiled. 'Sounds like Lesley,' I said.

'Why?'

'I taught her to drive.' I finished my coffee. 'Do you know where she went?' Piff thought for a moment, then she said: 'It'd be on that insurance form.'

'What would?' asked Robbie.

I stared at them.

'Her forwarding address,' said Piff. 'She had to write it down in case there was a claim, remember?'

Robbie got up and went across to an overflowing desk. He rummaged around in its drawers; then he found a piece of paper and brought it over.

'Spalding.'

'Spalding?' I asked.

'She's gone to Spalding.' He showed me the paper. It said *Graceland, East Fen Road, Spalding, Lincs.*

*   *   *

It was one of the worst nights I had ever spent. For a start, there were various lumps under my cushions. Investigating them, I pulled out a tractor, a kangaroo and two shoes (odd). Also several crisp packets; they weren't hard, just crackly when I turned. The Aga made me swelter.

I still felt drunk. I gazed at the tilting ceiling and tried to gather my thoughts about Barry. The unthinkable had happened. My son had a father. Did he call him Dad? I pictured Barry twirling him around, as Robbie had twirled his son; I pictured my own son clinging to Barry's chest hairs.

I knew so little. Barry was a boatman. Lesley had worked in a pub and smashed a car. Her shadowy life, years removed, was thickening up and growing clearer. Why had she suddenly fallen in love, after all these years of women's talk? I felt suddenly loyal to her female friends, those invisible Leicester house-sharers, as if Lesley had let the side down. What was so great, anyway, about this Barry bloke? What had he got that I hadn't?

I decided, turning on my slipping cushions, that I wasn't really jealous about Lesley; I was jealous about my son. Just because he could wield an oar, why should this man sit through my son's chicken pox? He'd had years of his growing-up; I could never catch up. He had taken him to school; Edward had held his horny boatman's hand. Edward knew no better.

Had they met in Leicester? Was her passion strong enough to uproot her from her convictions? Or had she brought Edward up here on holiday, and this Barry, muscles flexed, had pushed their boat onto the lake and grinned at her with his white teeth, toppling a lifetime's ball-breaking moaning?

Did my son love Barry? I wanted him not to, of course. Like a damsel in distress, he was waiting for the real thing: me. I was the hero of a magazine; I was poised to arrive in Spalding, in all my glory, and sweep him off his feet.

And yet part of me was nicer than this. I loved this unknown boy enough to wish on him a happy childhood, loving a man like I'd loved my father. This was soft; I blamed the drink. But I couldn't bear this Barry to be a creep; I wanted him just nice enough to have made Edward happy, but not as happy as I could make him.

*　　*　　*

Upstairs they were quarrelling. They had been talking in their bedroom, all this time but I had closed my ears to the rising murmurs and thuds. My parents had never quarrelled. I had lain in my room, next to theirs, and heard silence. In fact, they were silent most of the time. They were content, that's why.

I heard faint footsteps on the stairs. I was half-asleep. *As light as a feather*, said the butcher. I would never know the boy he had lifted—Terence, who would still be in a wheelchair now, wherever he was. I wished I could get him out of my mind.

Fingers touched my lips. I opened my eyes. The little girl was standing there, spectral in her nightie. Her face grew closer; I smelt spearmint.

'Your teeth are yellow,' she said. Her finger was pushing my gums back. 'That's plaque.

119

Why are you so old?'

'I'm not old.'

'Why are you wearing Dad's shirt?'

'I haven't got anything else.'

'Why not?' she asked.

'I've got nobody to look after me.' My eyes moistened with self-pity. Or perhaps it was the sight of her in her little white nightie.

'I've got a friend called Alice. Have you got a best friend?'

I shook my head. 'Nope.' I heard a thud, from upstairs. I wondered what had happened to the girl in the Bed and Breakfast. Why couldn't men and women be friends?

She said: 'I'm looking for Kanga.'

'He's here.' I leaned over and picked him up from the floor.

'It's not a he, it's a she.'

Abruptly, she took the kangaroo and left me.

*   *   *

I think I slept then. I was on a beach that I knew was Spalding, even though I also knew that Spalding wasn't near the sea. There was the old woman in the sequined jacket; she was searching for something. She called herself my mother but she was too skinny—my mother's legs were fat, I had realized that quite recently. She said: *'Someone here is making a sandcastle. They must be. I'll close my eyes and count to*

120

ten.' She wandered down the beach, waving her handbag, and called *'Cooee!'* When she left I saw the sand move, and a child pushed up his face. He had been buried, and his eyes and mouth were clogged. The sand below him, where his body was, stirred. He was getting to his feet. I watched the sand falling off him, and I then realized that Piff was standing at the Aga.

She was wearing a dressing gown and putting on the kettle. She turned and said: 'Are you comfortable there?'

'I'm fine.'

She paused. 'I'm sorry about the noise.'

'I can't hear anything,' I lied.

'Would you like some tea?'

'No thanks.' I wanted to go back to sleep.

Some moments passed. Then she said: 'His father was an alcoholic.'

I paused. 'We all like a drink.'

She didn't reply. I heard the rattle of a cup. Her voice came from the other side of the room. 'If Robbie died,' she said, 'I would die too.'

*　　　*　　　*

I lay still, willing her to leave. She did. I heard her footsteps on the stairs, heavier than her daughter's.

I pulled the eiderdown over my head and dreamed that Eleni was clattering up to my

121

coach. She wore her white boots and dragged three bull terriers behind her, on a lead. When she got to the coach she kicked them off; they fell back like skittles. I knew she was pregnant, though it didn't show to anyone else. That's why she had behaved like that. She got onto the driver's seat and tried all the levers. Suddenly the engine burst into life.

I woke up. There was a noise outside the window. I pushed off the eiderdown, ran to the door and opened it.

Outside it was dark. The icy air whipped away my breath. Somebody was starting up my coach. It jerked backwards; the street was full of exhaust smoke.

I rushed round to the driver's door and wrenched it open. Robbie sat in the seat, bent over the wheel.

'Fuck off,' he said.

I hadn't wrestled since I was at school. He was smaller than me but hard and springy. His knee butted my stomach; I gasped and coughed. I slid on a *Beezer* and lost my balance. He grabbed me, but I pushed him away. I was suddenly terribly angry.

'You can't leave them,' I shouted, 'you stupid git!'

I slapped him across the face, feebly. He jerked back.

Then I took the key out of the ignition—I must have been drunk, to leave it there—and climbed down.

I knew he would follow. I waited at the front door; my bare legs were freezing. He passed me with his head bowed. Then he picked up his jacket, which he had never bothered to put on anyway, and went back upstairs, to his bedroom.

CHAPTER ELEVEN

The next day was so bright and ordinary I thought it had all been a dream. The children sat in a row at the table and demanded Frosties; the kitchen had been mysteriously tidied. Piff and Robbie chatted about their day. He had to go to work—he was an engineer and only minded the CND office part-time. They discussed, companionably, who was going to pick up the stuff for the freezer.

I had a monumental hangover. Last night seemed a mirage; so did Spalding. Last night Robbie had tried to run away from home; this morning his wife was ruffling his hair. I felt I was in the thick of something I couldn't trust, like the undertow beneath the sea's current. I hadn't been in a proper home for so long; was this how people really behaved?

I suddenly had a new picture of my marriage to Eleni. It wasn't like this. It was like one of those mating dances you saw on natural history programmes. There I was, trying to please her, bringing her gifts, leaping back when she looked ready to sting. It had been somehow thin but strenuous; like an animal, I had lived on my wits. I had called that love, but now I wasn't so sure. What was love anyway? I thought I loved an eleven-year-old boy I had never seen. When had he had a bowl of Frosties from me?

Things were changing. I could hardly remember what the house in Croxley Road looked like. It, too, had been mysteriously tidied now; it wasn't mine any more. Nothing was, not even my coach.

I wondered if Eleni knew I had gone, and whether she cared. I tried to picture her with the leather-jacketed man and my mind went blank. Did he understand her better than I did? It alarmed me, that I could hardly remember her face. Piff was more real. It was as if I had never been married at all.

I said goodbye to them. They stood in the doorway with their arms around each other; from behind them, the children looked out. They reminded me of the Indian family in Leicester. I seemed to be always peering into other people's doorways.

*   *   *

It was 8.45. My money was low so I drove to a Nat West. I stopped outside and took my card

124

to the Autobank. Then something happened. I slotted in my card, the window slid back and then the screen said: *Please key your personal number.* I stood there, my finger outstretched. I couldn't remember it.

This worried me. Behind me, someone arrived and coughed. I moved away. I had to do something. So I went to a phone booth and rang the estate agents in Orpington—no trouble with their number. They were just opening.

'I'm looking for a house in Croxley Road,' I said. 'Are there any on the market?'

There was a long silence; it lasted four 10ps. Then the girl returned.

'Nothing in Croxley Road,' she said. 'But we've a very nice three-bedroomed house in Thresher Road, just round the corner.'

I put down the phone. The bitch. I felt so angry that, in a rush, I suddenly remembered all four numbers of my Autobank code. So I went back and withdrew some money. The notes were crisp and new; they came out warm, as if someone was baking in there. I couldn't afford them but they comforted me.

Then I bought two packets of Kendal Mint Cake, one for me and one for Edward: a memento of the Lake District for both of us. I bought a football too. I climbed back into the coach, feeling belligerent. Whistling *What is this thing called plaque,* I headed for the M6.

125

It was a grey day but I felt better once I was on the road. I always did. Just to see the miles flick past on the dial raised the old spirits. The only thing that felt normal to me now was my seat, with Bernie's greasy satin cushion wedged into the small of my back, the familiar arrangement of stickers on the side window, my ribbed steering wheel and the oft-ignored sign thanking me for not smoking. The speedometer was more familiar to me than my ex-wife's face. I had done a spot of housework that morning—emptying my ashtray, throwing out my Polo wrappers and crisp packets. I had bought myself a box of Kleenex. I wore clean clothes. I had bathed and shaved. These small things meant a lot to me by now.

The countryside flattened out. There were signs for Warrington and Wigan again. The farms changed from stone to brick; they looked sootier and meaner. Just two days ago I had noticed the opposite phenomenon.

Why had they gone to Spalding? Nobody went to Spalding. Reg ran a trip to the Flower Festival once a year but I had never been. Despite my seaside dream, I knew there was no beach in the vicinity for Barry's boats. He must have another business on the go. I tried to picture Lesley as a barmaid, and failed. How could that Lesley wear a frilly blouse and flirt with travelling salesmen? She hadn't taken

126

a sociology degree to pull pints. By now she must have changed out of all recognition; it wasn't just my son who was altering with the years.

There's a saying, isn't there?: *To travel hopefully is better than to arrive.* I slowed down to a steady 50 mph; the longer it took the better. I had no idea what I was going to do when I found them; what I had dreaded had happened. I wouldn't simply find a woman and a child. However hostile she might be, there was something incomplete about that sort of set-up. In some small way, even if just to change a plug, they might have needed me. But now I was driving towards a complete family. I had seen a lion family on TV. What did they do to a rogue male who appeared on their territory, smelling wrong? They tore him to bits.

The lorry in front proclaimed *Fresh Food Costs Less at Sainsbury's.* I sluiced my windscreen and nibbled some Kendal Mint Cake. I passed a car, it had wedding ribbons on it, and one had come loose; it flapped in the wind. Robbie's family had unsettled me. However detumescing—and I'm a bit of an expert on that—there was something about children that changed a couple and made them somehow . . . What was it? Human. As faulty as before but somehow weathered. Members of the human race. Oh I don't know. All I knew was that Eleni and I hadn't been like that. And, by now, perhaps Barry and Lesley were.

At eleven o'clock I stopped for petrol. I was well south of Manchester. I climbed down, grunting. My back ached. My coach was looking dirty by now—dust on its paintwork and mud, from country lanes, spattered above its wheels. For some reason this pleased me; it was proof that I was doing something.

But when I went in to pay they wouldn't take my card. The girl hesitated, reading something on her computer, and then she went over to the bloke at the next till. He looked at me as if I'd molested his daughter, then he stepped over and said: 'I'm afraid we cannot accept this.'

'Why not?'

'I'm afraid you'll have to pay by other means.'

Reg had frozen my credit. I was furious, of course—I had to pay with my own money. But in a weird way I suddenly felt normal. Until now I'd suspected that nobody had even noticed I'd gone. Eleni hadn't done anything about the house; Costas had sounded his usual benign self and had misunderstood me. I had felt forgotten by the world. I know that's illogical, when I'd only been away four days, but it's surprising how quickly, once you're adrift, you feel you don't exist.

I existed for Reg, all right. Settling back into my seat I chuckled out loud; and he could do bugger-all else about it.

*   *   *

I turned off the M6, travelling east, and stopped for lunch at a Happy Eater. My head still throbbed and I fancied a fry-up. Unreasonably I blamed Lesley for my drinking; if she hadn't moved away from Windermere I wouldn't have this hangover. You can be unreasonable when you're alone, can't you? There's nobody to contradict you. I could work myself up into a lather about Lesley; she had no idea. She probably hadn't thought about me for eleven years. Men were redundant, except for fertilization purposes. In fact, she had probably forgotten about those three or four episodes back in the mist of time. They hadn't been that memorable.

To tell the truth, my strongest feeling had been duty. She had seemed to expect me to perform. This might sound unchivalrous, but in fact it was she who'd suggested it in the first place. We'd seen a film with Oliver Reed in it and she said he always made her randy. Besides, we'd run out of coins for her gas fire.

I squeezed out some tomato sauce from its sachet. If Oliver Reed had decided not to be an actor but, say, a chiropodist, then Edward might not be alive on this earth.

My head spun. No, she had probably forgotten all about it. Women are always forgetting that it was a bloke who helped them to do something in the first place; I'd noticed that when I was a driving instructor. By now she probably believed she'd had Edward by Immaculate Conception. Years had passed in the company of women. But she hadn't reckoned on her hormones—up had popped Barry and she was back to square one, manwise.

My waitress was very young; she looked as pure as a milkmaid, with a face shiny as nature intended. Why couldn't a simple girl fall in love with me? She would bring me apple pie, as this girl did, and she'd say *If you died, I would die too.*

Eleni had seemed simple. Nobody could have called her an intellectual. She'd liked dancing and clothes and winning soft toys at fairgrounds. But looks are treacherous. She hadn't been simple at all. She had spent six years playing a series of such complicated games and manoeuvres that if she'd patented them she'd be a millionairess. *Trivial Pursuits*, I would have called them, if somebody else hadn't thought of it first.

There was a film where Alan Bates was a shepherd, and he wanted Julie Christie to marry him. Why? she asked. 'Because when you look up, I'll be here,' he said. 'And when I look up, you'll be here.'

I paid the bill and left, casting a last glance at the waitress. She smiled back. When I

130

looked up she had been there, but not for long.

I climbed into the driving seat. To my left, a ploughed field stretched into the distance. It was so large that it dissolved in fog. *Far from the Madding Crowd*; that was the name of the film.

*   *   *

By 2.30 I was driving into Spalding. Despite the flat countryside it was a surprisingly pretty town, with a market square in the middle. I had covered 240 miles today, from mountains to fens; I felt I was taking a geography lesson from my own son.

I parked in the square, went into the hotel and sat in the window seat of the bar, to get my bearings. Through the glass my coach faced me, nice and close. Its radiator was furred with dust; above it was the word OLVO. I wondered where the V had fallen off.

Behind me, two men were talking. 'Golf GTi, brand new, D reg,' said one. 'Vanished into thin air. Not a dickybird since last March. Had all my papers in it, my kid's birthday present, pile of letters I was going to post. Whoever it was, if I find him I'll blow him to pieces.'

'Probably on the continent by now. Quick spray job, new numberplates.'

'Right outside my house. What's the bloody

world coming to?'

I realized, with surprise, that I hadn't thought of my car for two days. The old bitterness rose. She had taken my house and my car. I couldn't even remember what my parents looked like, she had chopped them up with her scissors. My past was as vacant as my coach; I dragged it around behind me, and when I turned my head all its seats were empty.

I calmed myself down; this wasn't the way to greet my son and his parents. I needed all my faculties today.

The Golf man told me the way to East Fen Road. I backed the coach out. Exhaust fumes blew about and a woman, wheeling a pram, glared at me. I wanted to say: it's not my fault. And did she know what the petrol was costing me?

I couldn't imagine Lesley living at a place called Graceland. She must have come up in the world. The only Graceland I knew was Elvis Presley's home—as big as Buckingham Palace and covered in pillars. I'd seen photos. I drove through the suburbs of Spalding. Fields stretched out, flat and grey under a grey sky; here and there stood a bungalow and a row of collapsing greenhouses. In a farmyard stood an abandoned double-decker bus.

Funnily enough I didn't feel nervous. I must have used all that up, over the past few days. There wasn't a drop left. I had had so many shocks and surprises—the chopper bike in the hall, the demolished houses, the butcher talking about a wheelchair. My spirits had been so battered that I was drained of energy. I felt harder. I suppose it was the presence of another bloke. Last Sunday, when I'd seen a strange man coming out of my house, something inside me had died. Today there was another strange man in a house that should have been mine. I felt exhausted.

What could I say? That I was an old friend and had just popped in for a cup of tea? Perhaps she would kick Barry out; perhaps she would tell Edward I was his real father and we were going to start up all over again. (I wasn't too sure about this; I didn't think I really wanted Lesley.) We would settle down in Graceland and it was Barry's turn to go and live above Costas's electrical shop.

Perhaps Edward would fly into my arms and she'd relent and say that blood was thicker than water and I could have him now. I would drive him off and we'd both live above Costas's electrical shop. We wouldn't be short of videos. We'd watch *Back to the Future* together; I'd felt foolish watching it on my own. We'd eat takeaway curries out of foil containers.

It was 3.30. Barry might be out at work. Edward would still be at school. Perhaps Lesley and I would get it all sorted out before they returned and we'd finalize the arrangements over hot buttered toast.

My palms were clammy; otherwise I felt quite okay. I thought, for the hundredth time: What was Edward like? Would he like me? The houses had thinned out and I was in the open countryside now. Would I like him? I hadn't found a Graceland; I'd seen some other strange names but not that. In a country this flat, at least you could see where you were. The road was as straight as a ruler; down below, on each side, ran glinting ditches. Bare earth stretched out on either side, to the misty horizon. It seemed a depressing place to bring up a child.

Ahead was a row of cypress trees and one more building. I slowed down. It was a bungalow. Two old Cadillacs were parked outside. The sign said *Graceland*.

My heart raced. I drove a hundred yards further down the road and parked in a lay-by beside a bus stop. I put on my anorak, climbed down and sauntered back along the road, bending against the wind.

I heard the faint sound of a radio, but when I got to the bungalow I could see no sign of life. It was shabby. A chained dog barked at me, twice, then lay down again. I looked around. On one side was a garage; the music came from there. Another car stood in the garage, and when I moved nearer I could see a pair of legs underneath it.

I moved away, quickly. I didn't want to meet

134

Barry just yet. He was busy under the car; the radio was playing a loud Country and Western number and he couldn't hear me. *When you'd gone darlin'*, sang the singer, *my heart just lay down and di-i-ed.*

I went up to the front door and rang the bell. A minute passed. *I'm so blue-hoo* went the song. Nothing happened. The dog thumped its tail.

Then, near me, somebody appeared at the window. I jumped. It was female, and wore a turban and dark glasses. She had bare shoulders, and a towel wrapped around her.

For a moment I stood there and stared. Then I mouthed *hello*. Lesley waved back in a friendly way—almost playful, wriggling each finger. She moved out of sight.

The song stopped. I glanced quickly towards the garage, but from here it was blocked by one of the Cadillacs. My heart moved into my throat, I prayed he hadn't heard me. I needed to speak to her alone: after all, it really wasn't his business. My mouth had dried up; never before had my heart beat so fast for her. Why had she looked so pleased? Hadn't she recognized me?

Another song started. The door opened. She stood there, pulling off her dark glasses. It wasn't Lesley at all.

'Pardon my attire,' she said. 'But I was just under the lamp.' She blinked, and rubbed her eyes. 'You look all white.'

I cleared my throat, and paused.

She went on: 'Dunno why I do it.'

'Do what?'

She jerked her head towards the garage. 'Catch him noticing the difference. Go on, say I've got a lovely tan.'

She was about thirty, and pink.

'You've got a lovely tan,' I said.

'Trouble is, the bits round the eyes. Never mind.'

I took a breath. 'I'm sorry to disturb you, but—'

'Come in. I'm Shirley. Can't shake your hand or me towel'll fall off.' She showed me into the lounge. 'You come about a trailer?'

I paused. 'Not really. I'm looking for somebody called Lesley.' I sat down in an armchair. 'It was Featherstone but she's probably married by now and changed it.'

'Oh,' she said. 'Lesley.' She pulled off her turban and shook her head. Her hair was bleached yellow, with black bits underneath.

'You know her?' I asked.

'I knew her all right. The woman with the bust like Dolly Parton.' She paused. 'Shame that her middle was the same size.'

'Where is she?'

'They've gone now.' She jerked her head at the back window. 'They were in number 3. Back in a tick.'

She left the room. I went to the window and looked out. Four trailers stood in the back

136

garden. Cypress trees fenced them in. A concrete path led to some dustbins, and a greenhouse patched with hardboard, and an aviary full of budgerigars. There was no sign of life, except for a line of washing; overalls blew in the wind—*too late*, the legs kicked. *Too late.*

I had to picture Edward here now. He had lived in a caravan; I had to imagine everything all over again. My brain ached; I had to dismantle my old Graceland, with the pillars. It had never been real anyway. I had to shut it off, like scenery, and fix this new place in my head instead. I had done it so often recently I felt congested.

The front door opened and a man came in, wearing overalls and wiping his hands on a cloth. He stopped and looked at me.

'Sorry,' I said. 'I'm Desmond. I was looking for Lesley and Barry.' It sounded odd saying *Barry* as if I knew him.

The man said: 'You got any money for me?'

'What?'

'He owed me for a calor gas cylinder.'

Shirley came back into the lounge, transformed. She wore a pink leather miniskirt and a fluffy sweater; she had put on some make-up in double-quick time. She looked younger now, and much prettier.

'Jim,' she said, 'He's looking for —'

'He told me.' Jim was older than her. He looked worn out. 'Never paid for that glass either.' He indicated the back window.

'The kid broke his greenhouse,' she said. 'He didn't mean to, Jim, he fell against it.'

'Was he hurt?' I asked, alarmed.

She shook her head. 'He was playing with the dog.'

I looked out at the greenhouse, with its three panes of hardboard. My son did that. It suddenly hit me; I felt dizzy, and sat down again.

'How long were they here for?'

'A couple of years, wasn't it, Jim?'

He nodded, and went into the kitchen. I heard a tap running.

She indicated the kitchen, and lowered her voice. 'He only calls himself Jim because of Jim Reeves. His real name's Arnold. I found out when we got married. It was on the certificate.' She sighed, and lit a cigarette. 'This place drives me round the bend.'

He came back. She said: 'You remember Lesley.'

He nodded. 'A pain in the arse.'

She giggled. 'She'd sit here and give me these lectures about men. She could talk. There they were, at it day and night.'

'At what?' I hadn't meant to ask that. Now she would tell me about their vigorous lovemaking.

'Hammer and tongs,' she said. 'The fights they had.'

'Kicked the bloody cooker in,' he said. 'What about my grill pan?'

138

'We're used to it,' she told me. 'The types we've had here, you wouldn't believe. Ex-cons. Girls on the run.' She turned to her husband. 'That bloke who said he was a hypnotist. They came for him, too.' She turned back to me. 'Then this bloke hired a trailer, said he was in import-export, and when they broke the door down all these magazines fell out. Should've seen the photos—had a donkey in one.'

I froze. 'Did Edward see them?'

'Edward?'

'You know,' I said casually. 'Their kid.'

'Oh, Teddy,' she said. 'No, they'd gone by then.'

I relaxed. He couldn't be looking at pornography at his age.

'Why did they come here?' I asked. 'To Spalding?'

'He had this job at Geest,' she said.

'Geest?'

'The bananas.'

'Never liked that Barry,' said her husband. 'Poncing around without his shirt on.'

'At Geest, in the packing department,' she said. 'Then he was on the dole for a bit, then he worked at the swimming baths, as a lifeguard, until the cutbacks.'

Her husband looked at her. 'How do you know all this?'

She shrugged. 'Lesley told me.'

'What was she doing?' I asked. 'Where did, er, Teddy go to school?'

139

'She tried to set up this business doing horoscopes. She put cards in the newsagent's.' Shirley indicated her husband. 'She said he was a Scorpio, so that made him sex-mad.' She sighed. 'She wasn't much good at horoscopes. And there she was, going on to me about financial blooming independence.'

'What was their kid like? Teddy?'

'Smashing,' she said.

'Smashing's the word,' said her husband.

'He was just a kid, Jim.' She turned to me. 'He was great to have around. A real laugh.' She paused. 'Livened the place up.'

I sat still for a moment, taking this in. But I couldn't just sit there, doing nothing. 'When did they leave?' I asked.

'Three years ago.'

'Have you got an address?'

'Have we got an address?' said Jim. 'If we'd got an address I'd get me fifty quid back. And I'd be asking for inflation on top of that. Vanished into thin air, the four of them. Packed up one night and buggered off.'

I stared at him. Shirley ground out her cigarette. There was a silence, then I asked: 'Four?'

He nodded.

Shirley said: 'Her, and Barry, and Teddy and little Victoria.'

'Victoria?'

'Her daughter.'

I nodded, as if I knew. Another moment

140

passed. My head throbbed. 'She had a daughter?' I asked, just to make sure.

Shirley nodded.

'Here?'

'Well, in Spalding General.'

'She had a baby with Barry?'

Shirley laughed. 'I don't think she had any other offers.' She paused, and smiled dreamily. 'Gorgeous little baby. I can't have any, you know.' She started untucking her sweater.

'Shir—' said Jim.

'Can't have kids. Take a look at these scars.' She stood up and pulled down her skirt. I saw her belly.

'Shirl!' said Jim.

'I'm only showing him. We tried for six years, didn't we, Jim. I had this operation, and then another one.'

She sat down suddenly and started to cry.

Jim turned to me. 'What you do that for?'

'I'm sorry,' I said. I stood up. 'Better be going.'

Shirley wiped her eyes. 'You going back into Spalding?'

I nodded.

'Give me a lift, could you? Got to catch the shops and all our cars are bust.'

Jim asked: 'How're you going to get back?'

'There's the bus at six.'

He frowned. 'You take care of yourself.'

She grabbed her coat. I said goodbye to Jim, who didn't move. He was gazing at his wife.

141

In the front yard, the dog rose to his feet, wagging his tail. I went up to him and stroked him.

'Remember Teddy?' I asked him. He slobbered over my hand. I thought: my son has stroked this fur. He's slobbered over Edward, too.

Shirley said: 'Rinty got run over. That's a new one.'

*   *   *

She walked beside me up the road. Her perfume was strong enough to smell out here. She didn't seem surprised to see a coach. In fact, neither of them had asked me anything about myself, or why I was here. She climbed in and sat next to the driver's seat, across the aisle. It was such a grey day that it was already dusk.

'She did my horoscope,' she said. I climbed into the driver's seat. She turned to me. 'Said I'd meet a tall, fair stranger.'

'Oh yes?' I started the engine and tried to turn the coach in the narrow road. It took three goes, shunting to and fro.

'She said I'd do a lot of travelling.'

I felt vaguely uneasy, and didn't reply. We drove along the road, back towards Spalding.

'Smoke?' She lit a cigarette, and passed me one. Then she said: 'There's something I want to tell you.'

Warily I asked: 'What?' She wore the same sort of white cowboy boots as Eleni; I could see them out of the corner of my eye.

'I know where they went.'

I swerved towards the ditch.

'Watch it!' she cried.

I steered the coach back on to the road. 'You do?'

She paused, and dragged on her cigarette. Mist was rising from the fields; I put on my lights.

She spoke. 'See, I had this, well. This thing with Barry.'

She paused. Beside me, her cigarette glowed.

'I'd never felt like that before,' she said. Her voice grew soft. 'It all started when Jim went to the Elvis Convention. It was in Coventry. He got out all his gear, you know, slashed shirt, white trousers. They all try to look like Elvis, but quite honestly in some cases it's best not to try.' She paused. 'And, all the time, it was Barry who had it.'

'Had what?'

'What Elvis had. You've either got it or you haven't.' She paused. I drove through the fog. It had thickened up, I could hardly see the road. I'd heard about this happening in the fens; people got lost for days. 'Jim never found out, of course. He's been very kind to me, you'll never know. Nobody will. I was in a terrible state when I met him. But you can't

143

help these things, can you.'

'Can't you?'

'You ever fall in love? I mean really? So you can't eat? So you ache all the time? So when you see a car that's even the same colour as theirs you start perspiring?'

I paused. 'I don't know,' I said. 'Once, perhaps. A long time ago.'

'What happened?'

'I married her.'

She stubbed out her cigarette. Buildings loomed out of the fog.

She said simply: 'He made me feel alive.'

We arrived at the market square. I stopped the coach and switched off the engine. The shops had lit their lights. A schoolgirl, holding a violin case, yawned outside a delicatessen.

When I turned, Shirley was crying. She said: 'Got a hanky on you?'

I pulled out a Kleenex and gave it to her. She blew her nose.

'He wanted me to go with him but I couldn't.' She wiped her eyes, but then she started sobbing again. 'He'd just had a little girl, I couldn't do that to a family, could I? I couldn't do that to Jim.'

There was a silence. A woman came out of the delicatessen, took the girl's hand and led her away.

Shirley said: 'I missed my period the next month. I thought I was pregnant. But it never came to anything.' She blew her nose again

144

and stuffed the Kleenex into her pocket. 'Anyway, he gave me his address, so I could write to him. I did, for a bit. He didn't reply much, he wasn't a letter-writer. And then his letters stopped.' She paused. 'I'm just telling you, because of the address. Nobody in the world knows about it. I've never told anyone, before or since.' She paused. 'Nobody to tell, really.' She pulled a couple more Kleenexes out of the box and stood up. '15, Lyndhurst Road, Reading.'

I let her out of the coach. She looked up at me. 'I just wish he hadn't lied about his name.'

'Who?' I asked.

'My husband.'

And then she was gone.

CHAPTER TWELVE

I didn't drive towards the M1. I couldn't face the motorway. Motorways batter you. I wanted a homely, my-sized road.

I drove south out of Spalding. My backside ached; my spine ached. I re-arranged Bernie's cushion but it felt heavy now, as if it was filled with putty. Outside it was foggy. Trees loomed into the headlights and fell away.

Fathers would be coming home from work, now; doors closing. Jim would make the rounds of his empty trailers, looking through their windows. How many families had they kept safe, just for a short while? How many people were adrift, like me? Wives had told me things I shouldn't hear; they told me because they would never see me again. I wondered if my mother had spoken to anybody, after she had wept; I wondered how many times she had wept and I had never seen. She didn't pull up her jumper, like Shirley; she wasn't the sort to show her scars. What can men do, to make women happy?

I wondered who the woman had been, on the beach, and who she had been calling. My dreams had become so strong, I couldn't shake them off. Sometimes they rose up, like a belch, and I tasted a moment I had forgotten. Perhaps I was having a nervous breakdown. In my old life day had followed day and there were jobs to be done and things to be fixed. The week was pegged down by simple names like Bognor and Ramsgate and Luton. Roads unravelled in front of my steering wheel and I knew what I was going to find. I had kept my head down. A broken engine drew me like a magnet. Blistered woodwork called me; it beckoned me and my sander to keep us both busy, with no questions asked. Your whole life can be lists. And, in the moments over, there's this woman in the house who you call your wife, who needs something from the few parts of you which she thinks she knows.

146

I had a son and we were playing on the beach. He lay flat, squirming and giggling, as I heaped sand onto his legs. Soon they were like two plaster casts and he was trapped, all mine. Above us, gulls were blown about the sky, haranguing each other. There was a woman there; she had her back to us. I couldn't see her face but I knew we were married, and we were happy.

My hands felt the sand: on top, powdery and warm; underneath, clogged. My son's skin burnt in the sun, just like mine; I anointed him with Nivea. He wiped his nose with his gritty wrist. Helpless with love, I knelt beside him.

If.

If I'd had a child, everything would be different. Wouldn't it?

*   *   *

Eleni wore a black bikini tied at her hips with careless little strings. Her knees were sandy. Her father shouted something at her, in Greek, but she was walking along the beach and didn't hear.

I'm thinking of seven years ago. My mother had just died, taking the secret of her rock cakes with her. All my mates were getting married; instead of playing football on Sundays they took their kids to theme parks. I

147

was thirty-five, and lonely. I had just started work at Peckham Pride and that afternoon, on the beach at Hastings, I fell in love with Eleni and her family.

Perhaps they nagged, but I couldn't understand the words. Her father owned a wine warehouse in Lewisham and he had hired the coach for a works outing. There were lots of young blokes who all looked dark and related. They chattered and touched, not British at all. It was a cloudy day but nobody seemed to care. Arianna was there, and Maria, and the aunt whose name I couldn't pronounce, and Costas, his future wife still unknown to him. Zither music played on a cassette recorder; we speeded through the dour London streets. Their mother was already an old woman, in the Mediterranean manner; she sat in the front of the coach and crocheted. There were about twenty children but they didn't stampede about; they were shiny-haired and twittery, like starlings. In my mirror I could see Eleni; she sat close to her cousin Arianna, whispering; her hair was pulled up and fixed with orange combs.

On the beach the sun came out and the women unpacked the food. They patted a rug and included me; when I closed my eyes they were the family I had never had. Eleni pressed an olive into my mouth. How salty her fingers were! With her family as audience, she was bold and rebellious; she skittered off along the sand like a foal. I watched her. She was knowing and yet innocent; she flirted with the surf, willing the waves to touch her.

Smoke rose from the barbecue and stung my eyes. The women cooked; the men played with the children, it didn't seem to matter whose, they all belonged. Greek families are like that. Just for today, I belonged too. I rolled up my shirtsleeves and drank sour wine and was filled with contentment. We ate kebabs and Eleni's eyes met mine. After lunch everybody paddled, even Mrs Savvides, her mother. It was one of those days that you store in a larder, like something nourishing that will keep for ever so long as nobody opens the door.

On the way back everybody dozed, their faces fiery in the sunset. The children flopped like puppies and the cassette clicked off. Only Eleni stayed awake. I learnt her name then. She sat next to me, wriggling her toes in her peep-toed sandals. I could smell her suntan oil.

My hands felt big and manly on the wheel; she made me feel like that. Forty sleeping souls were in my care—I was new to coach driving, and the responsibility of them. She told me about the hairdressing salon where she worked, and how she'd once been on *Top of the Pops*.

'Who's been let loose on this?' she asked, touching my hair with her long red fingernails.

'Who's the butcher? Your girlfriend?'

'I haven't got a girlfriend.'

'Tell you what,' she said, after a pause. 'I'll do you for free.'

*   *   *

The next Wednesday I sat in the salon, helpless under her fingers. She tilted my head, ruthlessly, this way and that; she smelt of a perfume I'd smelt on other girls. In the mirror our faces were strangely private; when she turned away she became other people's but then she turned back and our eyes flashed, we were intimate.

She tapped her foot to the music; she looked restless and professional. She wore plum-dark lipstick today; snip-snip went her scissors as she hummed along to The Supremes. Her hair was reddish, and piled up. Only two meetings, and already we had seen each other at work; this made us familiar. She told me how trapped she felt, living with her sister. She wanted to get *out*, *out*, *out*, she mouthed to the beat. *Out.*

When she had finished we both sat back and looked. Then I grabbed her handbag, took out her lipstick and, on the mirror, scrawled a big, dark tick. It was true; she had given me a wonderful haircut.

She grabbed back the lipstick. I thought she was angry at me for blunting it—years later she would have been. But this time, this early, when we were new to each other, she leaned across to the mirror and scrawled three big XXXs. We smiled at our reflections through the graffiti, and I was lost.

*   *   *

Now my hair tickled my neck. For six years she had looked after it. Now I'd have to find a barber's shop. How much does it cost, nowadays, for a haircut?

*   *   *

I had pulled off the road. This frightened me—I didn't remember stopping, or turning off the engine. I was parked beside a dual carriageway; beside me, a car crept past in the fog.

I noticed with surprise that my ashtray was full. In the cubbyhole was a carrier bag; I had put the comics into it but where had I bought them? Which shop, in which town?

I didn't know how far I'd driven; the fuel gauge was three-quarters full. In my headlights I could see a hedge beside the road; somebody appeared to have tipped a rubbish bin over it. My watch said 6.30; I didn't trust myself to drive. I knew I wasn't alone. I paused, holding my breath, but I couldn't hear anything so I switched on the lights just to make sure the

151

coach was empty. The seats had a theatrical, expectant look; at each of the windows a little curtain was drawn back and hooked to the side, as if we were all waiting for something to begin. An empty coach isn't just empty; it changes, according to your mood.

Two more cars crawled by. I felt exposed, with my vehicle lit like a liner, and I switched the light off. The seats were swallowed up in the gloom. When my eyes got used to the dark I turned round again and looked at the rows of them, two each side. I thought of them occupied by my unborn children. I heard the rustle of whispers; was that a giggle? I couldn't see their faces, I didn't know their ages, but they were all a part of me and each one of them made a future. Despite Eleni's complaints we must have made love hundreds of times; there might even be a woman to come, though it was hard to imagine at this moment. All the possibilities made my brain ache. Blokes don't usually think like this, do they? It wasn't what you discuss down at the pub. I was probably off my rocker.

I was dead tired. There was no question of driving. So I turned off the headlights and made my way down the aisle, to the back of the coach. I felt as shaky as an old man in hospital. We kept blankets in one of the overhead racks, so I bundled up one as a pillow, wrapped myself in two more, and lay down on the back seat. It was narrow, and my nose was cold. A passing lorry shook the coach. I stuffed my knuckles into my mouth, and fell asleep.

*　　　*　　　*

I was going into a shop to buy Clearasil for Edward's pimples. It was the butcher's shop in Windermere but it had changed to a chemist's now, and instead of the lake around the corner I knew there was the sea. I could hear its murmur.

I said solemnly: 'My son will soon be a man.'

Somebody passed me a package, I couldn't see their face.

I took it and announced: 'The first pimple. Know what it heralds?' I sighed. 'Love. Poor little sod.'

Outside the shop I looked for him, but the street was empty. It was longer now, and stretched into the distance.

'Poor little sod,' I said. 'And pray, will any woman want him?'

I stopped and listened. I couldn't hear a sound except, somewhere beyond the buildings, the creak, creak of a pushchair. And when I looked down at my hands, there was nothing in them.

*　　　*　　　*

When I woke I thought: *Edward and Victoria.*

153

They were such quaint, old-fashioned names for a liberated woman—why had their mother chosen them? Her children weren't growing up amongst crinolines, it was all AIDS now, and rubbish in the hedges. My coach tours didn't take the rubbish routes, we took the scenic ones, but you couldn't fool me any more.

My mouth was dry and I felt irritable. Stupid woman. One father didn't exist and the other one, Barry, sounded randy as a tomcat— some father he made. Did she really think that their Christian names would keep her children safe?

To my surprise, it was 10.30 at night. I had cramp in my left shin. I needed to meet a human being and see if I could still behave normally; I felt I'd been alone for days.

I climbed into the driver's seat and started the engine. I pushed in Ricky Nelson. But the tape burbled and his voice slurred. *Hello, Mary Lou* . . . He sounded as if he was sinking into a tub of glue. *Goodbye, heart* . . . He choked to a stop, and when I tried to pull the tape out it had caught in the machine. I left it dangling. It swung, as I pulled into the fog.

I drove on until a sign loomed up, indicating Peterborough. I hadn't come very far at all.

*   *   *

I sat in an Indian restaurant in Peterborough, it was called Curry Paradise. I watched a

154

couple fondling each other. She was bigger than him and rested her cheek on top of his head; she adjusted her position as his hand slid up her thigh—I could tell he was doing this because he had a smug look. Sitar music played; the place was almost empty and as red as a womb. However much I ate there was still mounds of stuff in my dishes.

The woman giggled; the man nuzzled her neck. I'd had trouble making myself understood to the waiter; either I wasn't speaking clearly or he didn't understand English. I had half a lager instead of a pint, and a dish of something I hadn't ordered; it looked like dung and was sunk in transparent yellow oil.

When I couldn't stand it any more I stood up, went to the phone and dialled my number. I was going to tell her to get a move on with selling the house. Or, I just wanted to hear her voice. Or, I felt like getting her out of bed and making him annoyed. Or, I don't know.

There was no answer. I let it ring for several minutes. On the wallpaper beside me some numbers were scrawled in pencil. One was for mini-cabs, another was for somebody called Jock. Perhaps I should phone one of them instead; it wouldn't make much difference. A stranger would be kinder to me than my own wife.

Where was she? Perhaps she lay, legs locked with his, duvet over their heads, willing the phone to stop. Perhaps she was out. I had no idea where she would go, now. Her life had changed so completely; overnight she had become somebody I could hardly recognize. All these years she had been waiting for a man to make her into this new Eleni—houseproud, for a start. Maybe she could talk to him about the things I'd only feigned interest in—her ice-skating; Bernice at the salon where she used to work, who still made her jealous; which diet she should try next. I had only nourished a small part of her, as she had done me. I realized this now, but was it the same for everyone? Was Shirley and Jim's understanding deeper, even though she said the place drove her round the bend? I had been like Jim, tinkering with engines. There must be more to them than that. I hoped there was, or else everything became too thin to bear.

I paid the bill. My coach was parked in the empty shopping centre. A faulty streetlamp flickered. What now? For once in my life I wasn't sleepy. Besides, I didn't feel like dossing down on the back seat and being woken by housewives' stares.

I started the engine. Its first small coughs reassured me now, they were as familiar as my father's in the morning. My coach was becoming more human to me than people I saw in restaurants. I reversed out, with Ricky dangling. Some people call him Rick, I know, but he's always stayed Ricky for me. That was the end of him now, anyway—no more songs from Ricky.

*   *   *

I drove down south, and then I swooped up an overpass and joined the M25. The football rolled across the floor. London was an orange glow, out-glowed by the arclights above me. It was two in the morning and there was no traffic. I nearly turned left into London but cowardice stopped me. I couldn't face my dirty dishes in Costas's flat, and I'd forgotten what I'd left in the fridge. Then of course there was Reg. I'd lost my job for sure.

Out in Orpington, beyond that sleeping city, my own wife slept, deaf to my telephone calls. Perhaps she was murmuring into a male ear: *He wasn't up to much.* Mrs Selwyn's words. Perhaps she was nuzzling a male moustache and murmuring, like Shirley: *You make me feel alive.* On his oily, handsome, prat's face he had that smug look.

CHAPTER THIRTEEN

It was a fish and chip shop. Closed. Not surprising, really, at 3.30 in the morning.

I was parked opposite. I gazed at it, through

the sodium street lighting, and tears trickled down my cheeks. After four days I had caught Butler's cold; or maybe I'd got it from that dog, years and years ago, when I'd stood in Ardley Street. Kleenexes lay like blossoms around my feet.

Every mile, I'd been growing angrier. My nose was blocked and I was spoiling for a fight. How could this Barry dump my son in a trailer, surrounded by fog and pornographic literature? What sort of an example did he set, having it away with his landlady in front of a growing lad? Lesley was included in this irritation, for putting up with it. She'd never have let me get away with anything like that. Once, in a garage, I'd paused in front of a pin-up calendar and she had lectured me for hours. In my flat one day she'd felt the earth in my rubber-plant pot, pronounced it dry and accused me of insensitivity towards growing things. The nerve of it, when she was carrying my child. She flashed across my memory, bundled up like a Mongolian peasant and hectoring me about her needs. I couldn't believe I'd once been fond of her.

They obviously didn't live here. To tell the truth, I hadn't expected them to. This Barry was a slippery customer, him and his chest hair, and he'd probably given a false address. Why he deserved to keep his daughter, God and Lesley only knew. I had given up expecting things to be fair. Actually, I'd given up on my

158

own son. I was getting the flu; my bones ached.

Above the shop was a pair of dirty windows saying SOLICITORS: COMMIS IONERS FO OATHS, with two of the letters gone. The floor above that looked derelict. It was a small street, dwarfed, beyond the rooftops, by a Texas Homecare store. Little care had been lavished on these homes, in fact half the street was boarded up. If they had ever lived here— and I couldn't imagine Lesley frying fish—they had long ago packed up and gone. Everyone had gone: to Tenerife, to Sydney. To here and there. To somewhere else. I hadn't even bothered to get out of my coach.

Somewhere, far off, a dog was barking. It went on and on like that baby did, the baby I never saw again in the Bed and Breakfast. A police car slid past the end of the street, paused, and slid out of sight. It was the dead middle of the night and I was freezing.

What would you have done? Back in London my bed awaited me, but I felt too poorly to drive. So I steered the coach into the Texas Homecare car park, got out and peed in some bushes, got back in and pulled all the curtains closed, with my trembling hands. I pulled every curtain, all down the coach. My whole body was burning. Inside my clothes, insects were crawling over my skin.

I bundled myself up in the back seat—it felt cosier, with the curtains drawn, it felt more like my place. Sooner or later I fell asleep.

159

*　　*　　*

'Des darling!'

I jerked awake. Beside me, a woman was speaking to me. She was close and loving. All down the coach there were bright needles of light; at the far end, the windscreen blazed. My head throbbed and my limbs felt like lead.

She wanted me; I scrambled to my feet. For a moment I thought my mother had come to look after me, in my illness, but then I realized this couldn't be possible. It was Eleni; she had found me at last. No wonder there had been no reply to the phone.

I parted the curtain. The light blinded me.

'Les darling, have you got the keys?'

I blinked. The sun was so bright, it took me a moment to focus. Then I looked down and saw a woman standing beside a car. She was speaking to this person called Les, who was walking across the car park, carrying a kitchen sink wrapped in plastic. My eyeballs ached.

The car park was full; it was a beautiful day. Couples were going to their vehicles carrying pieces of homes—a flat-packed table, a bed headboard. They looked purposeful, as if they all knew they were going to somewhere safe. I'm all right Jack, they said. They all had homes to go to. It must be Saturday, DIY day. I had once been one of these people, but how quickly they had become an alien species!

160

Unwashed, with my stubbly chin, I was a vagrant now. I felt as separate as an animal in the zoo.

I had no idea of the time—11.00? 4.00? Even guessing hurt my head and I looked at my watch. 1.30. I tried to calculate the day of the week: Monday, the motel. Tuesday, Thing's couch. Robbie. Wednesday? Where had I slept then? The beginning of my long drive seemed clearer than the last few days. I looked longingly at the bushes where sometime this morning, in the dark, I had peed in privacy.

I climbed down from the coach, on bendy legs, and steadied myself against it. The metal was warm, it was a gorgeous day for October. No, November. Remember remember the fifth of November. My Dad, bending down to put a rocket in a bottle and straightening up, coughing. He had died of lung cancer.

I made my way, slowly, to the car park exit, pausing to let a loaded estate car pass me. I felt even worse today. If I leant against the wall, people might think I was just enjoying the sun. I closed my eyes and smelt frying; it made me nauseous but I walked around the corner and into the fish and chip shop. The vinegar made my eyes sting. Friday, that's right. It was Friday.

A West Indian bloke stood there, lifting a smoking casket of chips. I knew I was ill because I was seeing double. There were two

161

of him, doing different things. My head spun.

'Anywhere for a leak?' I mouthed. That wasn't the way to speak, but I was pleased to manage words at all. My lips felt swollen and dry; my skull felt stretched.

'Nope,' said the other one.

It wasn't one man, it was two. This particular one was sticking an 80p label over the sign that said *Jamaica Patties 65p*.

'My goodness gracious,' I twittered. 'Twins!'

They thought I was drunk. A child came in and ordered three doner kebabs. An old man sat at a table and a Space Invader winked at me, telling me to mind my words, chum, and keep my balance.

The second twin was saying something to me.

'Lousards,' he said.

'Pardon?' I asked.

'Lousards.'

'What?'

'Use ours.' He indicated the back door.

I went into a yard, where I found an outside toilet. Two cats, sitting on a corrugated iron roof, eyed me with pity from their superior position. Oh, to be a cat.

In the toilet I tried to gather my wits. I had to ask these men a question but I couldn't quite remember what it was.

I want my son. What do you mean, want? Want him for what?

I'm looking for Edward. Teddy. Eddie.

162

Who's he? You don't know? Fish or fowl? Animal or mineral, alive or dead?

I've lost my son. Lost him? Where? Down the pan?

I pulled the chain and realized, with surprise, that the only person I really wanted to see, to put my arms around, to rest my head against, to be comforted by, was my mother.

          *   *   *

I went back into the café and waited while they served a sudden rush of customers. If only I was hungry, there was a terrific menu—Pizza rolls, Southern Fried Chicken, something called Creole Fritters; cod and haddock too.

Then it must be my turn because one of the twins, whichever it was, he wore the blue t-shirt, said: 'Can I help you?'

The words came out in the right order. 'Do you know a bloke called Barry?'

'You want him?'

I shrugged. 'I might.'

'He a mate of yours?'

It tripped off my tongue: 'I'm Lesley's brother.'

He nodded. I nodded. His face swung closer to me, then receded. Somebody dropped some cutlery and it clattered like cymbals.

Then he said: 'He's gone, man.'

'Where?'

He drank from a can of Diet Pepsi. 'Saudi-

163

Arabia.'

His face loomed. The air pummelled me to and fro. 'Dear Christ,' I said. Somebody started the juke box. I raised my voice. 'They've all gone?'

He shook his head. 'Just Barry.'

'Did they live here?' I shouted.

He shook his head again. 'Nope. He was a pal of mine. Not a mate. A pal.'

Through my illness I realized: Barry must have had his letters delivered here, the slimy git, so Lesley wouldn't see them.

'Is Lesley still here?' I shouted. 'And, you know, the kids?'

He took out the casket of chips, shook them and put them back into the oil. They spluttered. 'Nope.'

'She's gone?'

He shrugged. 'Ask Hilda.'

'Hilda?'

'Her friend, Hilda.'

He dwindled away, telescopic now. I gripped the counter; his face swung back.

'Where does this Hilda live?'

'Round the corner. Above Lots o'Fun.'

*   *   *

I just made it to Lots o'Fun. It was a video arcade—or, as they put it, a Family Entertainment Centre. Above it, there were some flats. I went up to the side door. There

164

were only surnames on the bells—not even an H for Hilda.

I staggered into the arcade. It had a violent carpet, all blacks and oranges, worn grimy round the machines. The place was nearly empty but there was a lot of noise going on, bleeps and clatters, perhaps it was inside my brain. There was an alarming sound and one of the machines disgorged coins, as if it was having a haemorrhage.

A man sat in the Change booth. He was wizened like a gypsy and was reading *Amateur Gardener*. I grasped the counter, to steady myself.

'Have you seen a lady called Hilda?' I asked. 'She lives upstairs.'

'Upstairs?'

'There's flats upstairs,' I said.

'Are there?' He put his fingers on the page, to keep his place. 'Never looked.'

'What's the world coming to?' I cried. Where's your neighbourhood spirit?'

'Uh?' He hadn't heard. 'Hilda what?'

'Don't know.'

He scratched his nose. 'What's she look like?'

I paused. 'Don't know.'

He went back to his magazine. 'Well, then.'

*   *   *

I thought I might faint soon, so I found my way

165

back to my coach. Its curtains were still closed. The car park was still packed. All the people looked exactly the same ones as before. Time had ground to a halt. As I climbed the step, a group of people stopped and looked at me. A man called cheerfully: 'Can we all join in?'

I closed the door. Now I was home, I felt much worse. I staggered down the aisle, knocking against the seats, and fell on to my blankets.

*   *   *

When I woke it was dark and my throat was on fire. This was hell, I knew it now, and I was already dead. I lay, throbbing and burning, in my big metal coffin. In my bones the marrow had frozen; my body was shot through with icy needles. I was trembling so hard, the change in my pocket rattled.

I must be dying, because flashes of my past came to me, pulsing behind my eyeballs—the cracked concrete where I played with my Dinky cars, the lino in the bathroom, the shadow of the fire-tongs against the wall, where they frightened me. It frightened me, that I heard my money jangling.

Remember that song, *Poetry in Motion* (Johnny Tillotson)? I used to think it was all about a tree, not a woman: *Oh-a-tree in motion, see her gentle sway, way down on the ocean, never to move my way.* Wasn't I a wally?

I was only young.

Water, water. When had I last had a drink? A crowd would slowly gather round my coach, then somebody would break in and they'd find me; bones.

It's pathetic, but just then I started sobbing for my mother.

*   *   *

I got to my feet, tripping over my blankets, and made my way down the aisle. It stretched for ever. *The mile of the aisle* I said to myself, to keep up my morale. I hobbled along, snuffling.

The door handle was freezing. When I opened the door, icy air hit my face. *Oh-a-tree in motion* I hummed. It was my only comfort, to make a grunting sound in my throat.

The street was empty. I had no idea what time of the night it was. The fish and chip shop was closed. I knew, of course, that it had never been open. The lights, the noise, the absurd black twins, they had all been a dream. This was a dead street, bathed in lurid orange light. Anyway, who was it I was looking for? I kept humming, to remind myself I was alive. If I didn't have a drink of water I would die.

I managed to get to the end of the street, an epic voyage. I stood on the corner, swaying. Lots o'Fun was closed. I gazed at the dark window. In the gloom the machines looked as extinct as dinosaurs. Long ago I had imagined a man in that booth.

I looked up. All the windows were dark, and I didn't have the energy to raise my wrist and look at my watch. I was seized with a fit of shivering. I went on trying to hum: *Way down on the ocean, never to move my way.* Lifting my finger, I felt my wet cheek.

If Mum would come. I stepped backwards off the pavement and stood in the road. I lifted my head like a wolf baying at the moon and I bellowed, with all the power of my lungs:

'HILDA!'

*   *   *

Upstairs, a light was switched on behind the curtains. On the floor above, another light came on. I heard a window opening.

I didn't know how long I stood there— seconds or minutes or hours. My legs were buckling. I kept my eyes on that side door. A car passed, and the dog was still barking. Only that door could save me.

The door opened. In a blaze of light, a woman stood there. She was small and dumpy and she wore a dressing gown.

I gazed at her shape, halo-ed in brightness.

'Mum!' I cried.

And then I passed out.

CHAPTER FOURTEEN

When I woke I was lying in bed. Beside me, football stickers were sellotaped to the wall. It was a small room, narrower than my coach. Somebody had taken off my trousers, shoes and sweater and laid them on a chair.

Daylight glimmered through the curtains. My head felt clear. Mentally, I felt my body from top to bottom. Frail, but better. I looked at my watch: it was 2.00.

I must have drifted off again because the next time I opened my eyes I heard a rattle; the door was open and the woman was coming in, carrying a tray.

'Feeling better?' she asked. 'How about a nice cup of tea?' She pulled up a chair and sat down. 'I went mad and made us some scones, just in case.'

I nodded, and moved to a sitting position.

'Let's make you comfortable,' she said, and plumped up my pillows. 'Sugar? Lucky it's Saturday, so I don't have to go to the office.'

'Where do you work?'

She passed me a cup. 'Gas Board. For my sins.'

I sipped the tea. It spread through my limbs, warming them. It literally brought me to life.

'Go on, let's be wicked,' she said, passing me a scone. She had already buttered it.

'Delicious,' I said truthfully, my mouth full of crumbs.

'There's more in the kitchen. And flapjacks. You like flapjacks?'

I nodded.

'What you looked like, you poor thing,' she said. 'You've no idea.'

'You're Hilda?'

She nodded. Then she leant forward and touched my cheek. 'Colour's coming back.'

'How did you get me here?'

'The man upstairs helped me.' She smiled, roguishly. 'Tongues'll be tattling.'

She was rather plain, with waved brown hair, like women used to have, and a suety sort of face. Have you met people, and you don't know how old they are? She reminded me of a girl at school, who had already looked middle-aged.

'Sorry to land on you like this,' I said.

'No problem. I didn't have many plans actually. Nice to have some company.'

I knew I should explain why I was there, but just for the moment I didn't have the energy. From what I could see, she didn't seem curious. She sat there, working her way through the scones and smiling at me. I can't tell you how comfortable I felt—comfortable and sleepy. It seemed I had been driving for centuries.

'Ready for those flapjacks?' she asked.

I nodded. 'Yep, sirree.'

As she got to her feet I indicated the football stickers, and the *Star Wars* poster above them. Two of its corners had come unstuck, and curled from the wall.

'Your son's?' I asked.

She giggled. 'Oh no. I'm footloose and fancy free.' She brushed crumbs off her lap. 'They're Edward's.'

I paused. Then I said: 'Edward?'

'A boy who lived here.' She went to the door. 'This was his room.'

CHAPTER FIFTEEN

All that Saturday afternoon I lay in my son's bed, drifting in and out of sleep. When I opened my eyes, there were his blurred Liverpool stickers. I vaguely chastised him for not supporting his local boys, but hours later, when I resurfaced, I realized that in those days he was too young to know he lived near the Arsenal ground. Each time that I'd met him—well, almost met him—he was growing older. With Mrs Selwyn he'd had a nap; four years later he had romped with a dog and broken a greenhouse. I was close to him now—so close that I buried my face in his pillow.

I'd had a little bedroom too, like this. Far away, I heard the sound of a Hoover. It echoed down the years. Someone was busy, putting

171

everything to rights. I stayed tucked up, nothing on my mind. I metaphorically sucked my thumb. Hilda was humming in the kitchen; I smelt baking.

When it grew dark she came in and drew the curtains, keeping us safe.

'One-day flu,' she said. 'That's what it is. Lots of girls at work've had it.'

Wasn't that comforting! And I thought I had been dying. She reminded me of an aunt of mine, who had called the war 'a silly bother'. Everything was going to be all right.

'It makes a change, to shop for two,' she said. 'I've bought us a gorgeous piece of lamb for supper, and made a crumble, and you're not to get out of that bed.'

'Let me,' I whined. 'Go on.'

'All right. You can come into the lounge, as long as you stay wrapped up. Now, about these clothes.' She lifted up my trousers. 'Polyester mix, I can run them through the machine. Number 4. Strip off.' She put her hands over her eyes and chortled: 'Promise I won't peek.'

She took away my clothes and I lay under the sheets, bare as a newborn baby. The room was warm. I felt whole, from my fingers to my toes. A delicious smell drifted in from the kitchen and I heard the murmur of a radio. No woman, since my mother, had really liked cooking for me. Women had made me meals, of course, but that was different. I mean cooking.

I closed my eyes and thought of Eleni. Dying, or one-day flu, had put her into another life and it alarmed me that I could remember so vaguely. She had liked nibbling things out of little tubs; we were usually out of tempo with each other and hardly ever sat down to a proper meal. Even then she'd be on some fad of her own—Lean Cuisine or something from a Jane Fonda book. She might buy me a pork chop but as she turned it under the grill she wore a preoccupied look, a bit distasteful, as if there was something flabby about it that reminded her of me. It was always undercooked.

You might ask: why didn't I cook my own chop? Lesley would ask that. But that's not what I'm talking about.

I lay, naked between my son's sheets. I was enveloped in peace. Hilda demanded nothing of me; I had never met a woman like this. It suddenly seemed so simple. My past, in retrospect, had been one long obstacle course, sweetly turfed but with treacherous pits underneath, waiting to break my leg at the ankle.

She ran me a bubble-bath and I lay there, reading one of her paperbacks. It was the story of a shy nurse who won the heart of the world's most distinguished surgeon; on the cover he had film star looks and a suntan. Hilda had a lot of books like that, but when I teased her she took offence and hid them in

173

her bedroom.

I dressed in my clean clothes; they were warm. She tucked me up on the lounge settee. I realized that she had put on some lipstick; she wore a dress with a frill at the collar.

Now the nursing was over she was owed an explanation. I said: 'I came here to find Lesley.'

She got up and went into the kitchen. I heard clatterings.

I raised my voice: 'You know, Lesley.'

She came in. 'Five more minutes, to crisp up the potatoes.'

'Lesley Featherstone,' I repeated.

'I know. I heard you.' She took away my ashtray and tipped its contents into the bin, rapping it against the sides. 'That disaster area.'

'Was she?'

'You should know.'

'Not really,' I replied. 'It's only, well, an old business matter.'

She turned round. 'Is it?'

I nodded. 'She's got something of mine. That's all.'

She didn't reply. Her face went pink; she looked quite pretty then.

'Mustn't keep those potatoes waiting,' she said, and hurried into the kitchen.

Why had I lied? Well, half-lied. I don't know.

Supper was wonderful: roast lamb, three sorts of vegetables, roast potatoes, the kind of rich dark gravy nobody makes any more. She kept re-filling my plate. We sat side-by-side on the settee, watching an old film with Katharine Hepburn in it—the one where she plays a golf pro.

'Isn't she beautiful,' Hilda kept sighing.

We ate the crumble and, after a brief struggle, she let me scrape out the bowl. Afterwards she suggested cocoa but I stood up.

'I'm taking you out for a drink.' The food had been lavish, but lacking an alcoholic dimension. Besides, I wanted to take her out.

She stood up, flustered. 'Shall I change?'

'You look lovely.'

She went pink again, and touched her crucifix—it was a tiny gold one she wore round her neck. She reapplied her lipstick and we went downstairs.

*   *   *

Time was still disjointed, as it had been all week, and my illness had shuffled it again, like jigsaw pieces that take longer to reassemble. Surprisingly, it was only 9.30. We walked past the fish and chip shop, all lights and people now. I showed her my coach. It looked strange,

175

sitting in the empty car park, as if I'd never driven it. The closed curtains gave it a mysterious air. I told her that since Monday I must have driven a thousand miles.

'Fancy that,' was all she said.

We went to a pub at the end of the road. I was getting fond of this neighbourhood. It was a maze of little streets but she said it was all going to be pulled down to make a shopping mall, and she would have to find somewhere else to live.

I asked her about her parents. She said she saw them each Sunday but she had put tomorrow's visit off, on account of me.

'If I brought you along,' she added, with a little laugh, 'they'd get all the wrong ideas.'

I parked her in an alcove—'parked' was somehow the word—and went up to the bar to get the drinks. Beside me, a man was sitting on a stool. When I had ordered he turned to me and grinned.

'How's the hangover?'

'Pardon?' I said.

'It was me who carried you upstairs.'

'I wasn't drunk,' I protested. 'I was ill.'

His face looked skinned, like corned beef and his eyes were bloodshot. They were sunk into his skin, like Reg's. 'Staying with our Hilda, then,' he chuckled.

'What do you mean?'

'Our Hilda,' he said. 'Stuffing one end because nobody wants to stuff the other.'

It took a moment for this to sink in. I felt sick. Then I hit him.

Actually, I slapped his cheek. He wobbled on his stool, staring at me. Then he took out his handkerchief and wiped his mouth.

My hand stung; I think I'd hurt myself more than him. I paid for my drinks, with a trembling note. The landlord hadn't noticed anything. Avoiding everybody's eye, I made my way back to Hilda.

She gazed at me. 'That was Dennis,' she breathed. 'Why did you do that?' Then she giggled. 'Defending my honour?'

'Yes,' I said.

*   *   *

In less than a week I had hit two men. I'd never raised my hand to anyone in my life before; what was coming over me, in my middle-age? If I punched anyone, it should be the man who had stolen my wife.

In less than a week I had lost my job. I had joined the CND. I'd had a wet dream. I'd nearly died. I'd almost found my son.

*   *   *

'I'd put a postcard in the newsagent's,' she said. '*Second girl wanted, non-smoker, to share flat.* So she turned up, with these children in tow. She hadn't said anything about them.

177

Gorgeous little girl, Victoria, she was into everything—that age. I think they're lovely then, don't you? Bit of a handful, but still. And Edward. He was lovely too, freckles and everything. He said *"I'm nearly nine, how old are you?"* What a character. He snuggled up to me, that first night. I'd put him to bed, in the room you're in. He'd got these two carrier bags, with his toys in them. He'd lost his pyjama bottoms. Honestly, those poor kids. She wasn't fit. He said his Superman robot was broken but his Daddy was going to fix it.'

'Daddy?'

'Somebody called Barry. I never saw him, Lesley had just walked out on him, apparently. Anyway, little Edward said his Daddy was away for a few days but he could fix anything, he was the best Daddy in the world, he'd made him a go-kart but that was in Spalding, they couldn't fit it in the car, and he'd made him a bow and arrow, a special one out of willow wood because it bends, his Daddy knew all about that. And how he'd worked on the oil rigs for a thousand pounds a day, and how he'd been a spy and gone to America and met all the actors in *Star Wars*—'

'He hadn't!'

'No, but Edward didn't know. It was so sad, Dezzy, because he kept saying his Daddy would come home at the weekend but he didn't, and then he said he'd come home for Christmas and bring him a present but I knew

178

he wouldn't because he was in Saudi-Arabia. He did send him a t-shirt but it was too small.'

She paused for a moment, her needles clicking. She was sitting in the armchair, knitting, and I was lying on the settee. There was a wheeze, and her cuckoo-clock opened. It was midnight.

'Les smoked. She hadn't told me that, either, but I didn't mind. I thought we could be friends. I said to her once: *"It's a bit of a giggle, isn't it? Girls together."* She put on this solemn voice. *"We're not girls together, Hilda. We're women together."* Honestly!' She paused, and picked up a stitch. 'She said she was through with men, they were never any good, she always picked the wrong ones.'

'Did she?' I asked.

'It was fine at first.' She lowered her voice. 'In the, you know, the bedroom department. But then they thought they owned her, she said. They dominated her.'

I stared. '*They* dominated *her*?'

'She said they just wanted her for her body.'

There was a silence. I hadn't. If anything, it was vice versa.

She went on. 'She said they didn't want to know the Lesley in her.'

I thought: did she want to know the Desmond in me? I didn't speak.

Hilda went on: 'She'd had a rough time, she said. She'd fallen for this Barry chap, but he was everything she despised. She said it was

179

like a disease.'

'Did you know about Oliver Reed?' I asked.

'What?'

'She fancied Oliver Reed.'

She shook her head. 'Didn't know that. She said she could only fancy men who she had nothing in common with. She called it something hoity-toity. I remember, we were having our Horlicks.'

'Called it what?'

'It was the title of one of her books. She had tons of books.'

'What did she call it?'

She rolled her eyes. '*The Perversity of Sexual Desire.*'

I paused. 'I know what she means,' I said.

'Do you?' She looked up.

I didn't reply. 'Go on,' I said.

'She always had a theory for everything, she was such a know-all, but look what a mess she was in.'

There was a moment's silence. The needles clicked.

'Where did she meet him?' I asked.

'Don't know. They were in the Lake District together, I think, then Lincolnshire. Then they came to Reading.'

'Why?'

'She'd heard of a therapist here.'

'A therapist?'

'It was a woman who did trance dances.' Hilda giggled. 'And they used to bang pillows

180

about and pretend they were being born.'

'But they were born.'

'Born again. She tried to explain to me but *Crossroads* was on. Anyway it didn't work out.'

'Why not?'

'They all quarrelled. Then they had therapy about that. She used to come home and tell me all about it. And there I'd be, trying to make the children's tea. She knew all about maternal bonding, as she put it, but could she bake a bakewell tart?'

We sat there, considering this. I had a momentary flash of comradeship for Barry, kicked out, like me, after he had reproduced. Was it the praying mantis that ate her mate? This didn't last, however. I was more worried about my son.

'What happened to the children?'

'School's a godsend, isn't it. Even nowadays.' She stopped, and gazed down at her knitting. It was a cardigan, for her mother. 'They were so lovely.'

'The children?'

She nodded. Then she pushed a lock of hair out of her face. 'Sometimes I think life's just a tiny bit unfair.'

'You think so?'

'Don't you?' She raised her face. Her nose was shinier now. 'I loved those kids.' She paused. 'Should have heard her yelling at them.' She bent her head, again, over her pink wool.

181

*　　*　　*

When I woke next morning I couldn't remember where I was. Somebody was humming in the bathroom. I heard the muffled grunt of a geyser. It was Sunday; I was in Reading.

I dozed, and had a vision of Hilda and me. We were propped up in bed, side by side. We wore pink cardigans and were both reading different books by Dick Francis. I thought: there are worse ways than this, aren't there, to live with a woman?

Look what a mess this Perverse Thing Called Desire had got me into. The two biggest messes in my life. To be quite frank, had it been worth it? I would say, by and large, no.

Looking back on it, the whole business seemed fraught with embarrassment and danger. Knees and chins jabbing into the wrong place; the fear of offending somebody by yelping with pain. The teeth, the tongue, the toenails, all met unexpectedly. The sudden attack of wind. The lurking suspicion that one or other of you might be getting bored. The bed-creaks, like pistol shots. The painfully-trapped hair. The obligation to do it differently this time, in a new and cramp-inducing position, and knowing I had to get up at six the next morning. The muffled

182

endearments that came out silly. The terrible fear of it all being over too quickly—I had found the silent recital of the World Cup squad helped this, but not always; not by any means. The dogged grind when I wanted to lie there, panting like a spent porpoise, but more, sometimes a great deal more, sometimes a full quarter of an hour more, was required. The effort of keeping this effort unapparent. The awkwardness, when you half-opened an eye and there was another eye, opened, jammed close.

The stickiness. The sudden, dizzy loneliness, like vertigo.

*   *   *

I dozed again, and saw my son, mooching around these streets—his neighbourhood, and mine too, by now. Outside Lots o'Fun he dawdled, longingly. He hop-scotched down the pavement, past the two derelict shops and the yard that sold reconditioned fridges, down to the chip shop to buy a Jamaican pattie. The same sun shone on us both.

I got up and opened the curtains. It was a grey day.

*   *   *

'They stayed here a year,' she said. 'Until last autumn. And then we fell out. Quite honestly,

183

Dezzy, I wasn't sorry to see her go.'

We were sitting at the table, formally, eating poached eggs. She was the first woman I'd ever met who believed in breakfast. She made poached eggs the proper way: white, humped moulds—like flattened breasts, I would have thought, if she wasn't there. When pressed with a fork, they yielded and spilled.

'Gosh', I said, 'my mother made them like this.' Then I asked: 'Why weren't you sorry?'

'She wasn't the easiest person to live with. She was always dissatisfied.'

'Was she?'

'She said it was me, but quite frankly I think she was dissatisfied with herself. She'd make these little remarks, I didn't understand this, I didn't understand that, I'd forgotten her muesli.' She mopped up her egg. 'Why should I remember to buy it when she'd been sitting on her backside all day?'

I laughed. 'Sounds just like marriage.'

'She said she could never live with a man, but I don't think she could live with a woman either.' She munched her toast, thoughtfully. 'I'd been quite happy till she came along. Really I was. But then she told me I shouldn't have been. I should have been changing my life. I suppose I should've been having two illegitimate children and living off the social security.' She stopped. 'That's unfair. I didn't mean that. I don't know what I mean, she got me all confused.' She picked up her crusts and

184

sucked the butter off them. 'It's silly, but I miss her. She made me—well, see things differently. And we did have some laughs.' She paused. 'I miss the little ones too.'

There was a pause. Then I asked: 'Did Edward have asthma?'

She stared at me. 'How do you know?'

I shrugged my shoulders. 'Just genius.' I polished an imaginary lapel.

*   *   *

I hadn't asked, yet, where they had gone. This might seem daft. But it wasn't nice, to go on cross-questioning her about someone else when she had made such a terrific breakfast. I should be asking her about the Gas Board.

She told me, over our final slice of toast and dark, thick home-made marmalade. She worked in accounts. On Tuesday evenings she went to Portuguese Conversation classes, and on Thursdays she went bowling with a girl called Cynthia, who worked in accounts too.

I helped her with the washing-up. She told me she was going to mince the leftover lamb and make us a moussaka.

I dried a cup and said: 'Really, I should be pushing off.'

She swung round. 'But what about lunch?'

I said she had been awfully kind, but I couldn't impose on her hospitality any longer. I ought to pop off and settle this little business

185

matter with Lesley, wherever she lived.

'I don't know,' said Hilda.

*   *   *

I nearly dropped the cup. 'What do you mean?'

'I don't know where she's gone.'

I stared at her. 'But she must have left a forwarding address.'

'She didn't get many letters.' She pulled out the plug; with a gargle, the water drained away. 'She wasn't close to her parents, I don't even know where they live, and she didn't have many friends.' She sniffed. 'She could at least have told me, but she wasn't terribly considerate.'

After a moment I asked: 'But what about school and everything?'

'She took Edward out at half-term. I know she was going through a crisis, but still. She could have phoned.'

I stood there, rooted to the kitchen floor. I felt a wave of bitterness against everybody—even Hilda's stout backside, in its tweed skirt. I was being sucked down the old hole of exhaustion. I glared at her *Greetings from the Algarve* tea-towel—fancy bothering to frame it!

I croaked, loudly: 'You can't even bloody well get in touch with her?'

'Don't!' She turned round; her face had reddened. 'Don't shout!'

We glared at each other. In the next room the cuckoo-clock struck.

She said: 'Even if I did know, I jolly well wouldn't tell you. Not if you speak to me like that.'

I shuffled towards her, a step. 'I'm sorry,' I mumbled. 'You don't understand.'

'I do understand,' she said. 'I'm not a complete ninny.'

I should have explained then, but I didn't. I just said: 'It's not like that.'

'Actually, I think it's ever so romantic.' She turned away and started rubbing the draining board with a sponge. 'Searching for her through thick and thin, in your great big chariot. Did you ever see *A Man and a Woman*, with the windscreen wipers going, and him driving through the night to get to her, oh it was lovely, remember that music, da,da,da, da-da-da-da-da da da da-da-da . . .' The hum died away. She scrubbed, vigorously.

'I told you, Hilda,' I said. 'I couldn't care less about Lesley.' My voice rose. 'I don't even like her much! I hardly know her!'

There was a silence. She squeezed out the sponge, thoroughly, and put it back in its plastic holder. This was the moment for me to tell her about Edward, but I couldn't. She would get the wrong idea, just as Eleni did; just as that bloke Eric did, years before. I put away the tea cup. She would think I was like Reg—a dirty bugger.

187

She peeled off her rubber gloves and laid them on the windowsill to dry. The sun had come out.

'She'd bought an old van, goodness knows how,' she said. 'An old banger. The morning after we'd had words, she packed up her stuff, and the children's stuff, and she was off to join her sisters.'

'*Sisters*?' I stared at her. 'She had sisters?'

'Not that sort of sisters, silly billy.' She pulled a face. She looked better now; her colour had returned to normal. 'Her sort of sisters.'

'The sisters at Greenham. You know. Those women.' She untied her apron and hung it up. 'The women at Greenham Common.'

CHAPTER SIXTEEN

'I used to go camping with my Dad,' I said. 'To give my mother a break. We had this tent for two, and I mean two. Not like these through-lounges they have now, and these perspex windows and car ports and roof extensions—'

'Don't be daft,' said Hilda.

'Well, anyway. We went to the woods outside Eastbourne, where the trees run down to the sea. Funny how it's always sunny, isn't it, when you're young? He made me a bow and arrow, it's not willow you should use, it's hazel.

Begging Barry's pardon.' I paused. 'We'd walk for miles, and then he'd sit and do the crossword while I climbed the trees, and he'd be whistling.'

'Probably because he'd got away from your Mum.'

'That's not true!'

'What makes you so sure?'

'Hilda, I was their son!'

Her needles clicked. 'My parents hate each other's guts.'

'Don't say that!'

'Why not? They only stick together because they were too cowardly to leave each other, and now they're too old.' She sniffed. 'He only speaks when he wants her to pass the ketchup.'

'How terrible.'

'You don't think it's terrible, when you're little,' she said. 'Me and my brothers didn't. You think it's normal.'

Trees lined the road. The sun had come out. As we drove past, the sunshine flashed between their trunks, on-off, on-off, like morse code. I was deaf to their messages. I fixed my thoughts on my father, whistling in the woods.

It was eleven that Sunday morning and the weather had turned cold. Hilda was accompanying me to this Greenham Common place, where the peace women camped out. I'd seen them on the TV. She was coming, she said, because Lesley had nicked her quartz alarm clock and she wanted to get it back.

189

Neither of us had high hopes of finding Lesley there—who would sleep rough for a year with two children? But somebody might know where she had gone.

The best Daddy in the world. Mine was, of course. Each man is, to his own son. What right had Barry to be the object of such adoration? Hilda said that children saw the truth, but I knew they lied. They had to lie to themselves; they had to make some faulty couple into the best parents in the world, because that was all they'd got. Barry was all my son knew. Even a father who disappeared to Saudi-Arabia was better than a father who had never turned up in the first place.

My son was slipping away from me. He had never known me, anyway; I'd never made him a bow and arrow. What right had I to him? From this absent boy I had constructed my own property, my own salvation in this—as they say in church—my Hour of Need. He wasn't a real son, he was some picture postcard equivalent of one. It was like people pretending that thatched cottages were a true picture of England. On my coach tours, that was the England we saw—Stratford, the Cotswolds. We fooled ourselves, of course.

That frosty morning, the first morning of winter, I knew that sons had to lie about their fathers. How? Because I'd just been lying, myself.

190

                    *   *   *

'Ugh,' said Hilda, shrinking in her seat.

We were driving past a high wire fence—the perimeter fence of the missile base. In front were various heaps of plastic, sort of tents, and hunched shapes sitting around in the smoke.

'How could they?' she muttered. 'The mud!'

I parked the coach further up the lane, and touched my CND badge. Like the Peckham Football Club, one sex only was welcome here; I knew that from the TV. But perhaps this badge made me an honorary member.

A woman stepped out from behind a gorse bush and walked up to us. She was bundled up in men's clothes. I opened the door for her.

'Great!' she called. 'Where are they?'

I stared at her. 'Where's who?'

She had an American accent. I thought her hair was grey, but on closer inspection it was speckled with dandruff. She gestured at the coach.

'Everybody. I'm real pleased there's so many.'

I turned round, and gazed at the empty seats. 'What do you mean?' I asked.

She frowned at me. 'You from Exeter?'

I shook my head. 'No.'

'Ah.' She looked at the coach. 'I was so pleased. We were only expecting a few.'

'I'm sorry,' I said. Now she was near I saw that it wasn't dandruff in her hair, it was wood-

191

ash.

Hilda buttoned up her coat. 'Excuse me, do you know somebody called Lesley Featherstone?' she asked.

It made a change, for somebody else to ask this question. It made Lesley real again.

But the woman hadn't heard; she was walking back towards the camp fire.

*   *   *

There were lots of Lesleys there, but none of them the right one. By lots, I mean they looked like her; I even saw the odd bobble-hat. They sat huddled round the fires, bundled up like crones. One of them smoked a pipe. Living outdoors had not only aged them, it had desexed them; they weren't like women at all. None of them took any notice of Hilda and me, as we edged our way through the bushes, past their rumpled nests, flimsily roofed with plastic, past their clothes hung, out to dry—or, in this weather, to stiffen. I averted my eye from their sleeping bags, so rudely exposed. They reminded me of my own belongings, flung out into the open to be gazed upon by strangers. But these women had a choice. This time last week, I realized with surprise, I was walking up my own street for the last time.

Hilda gripped my arm. 'I don't want my clock back, actually,' she confided. 'Its insides kept falling out.'

192

She squeezed my arm. I felt uneasy; it must be this place. It was odd to be amongst so many women who hadn't tried to make themselves attractive. Hilda, at least, wore matching boots and handbag.

Lesleys had come and gone, we heard. Lesley from New Zealand; another one; somebody called Les but the woman who remembered her had gone, now. None of them remembered our Lesley. We trudged through the mud. It was mostly Hilda who asked, virgin to sort-of-virgins. They weren't alike, she and these peace women—God knows there was little resemblance—but they were similar in that I didn't feel pulled, as a bloke, into some sort of battleground. Funny how, when I thought about women, military words cropped up. Eleni had called her make-up 'war paint'.

We moved out of the mud, onto some yellowed turf. Tut-tutting, Hilda took out a handkerchief and rubbed her boots. Through the fence I could see no missiles, jutting like male members into the sky. All I saw was drab, wintry countryside. Hilda didn't know where they were kept, nor did I, but a blue-nosed woman in a beret told us that all the nuclear warheads were kept underground.

'Like marriage,' I joked. 'You don't realize they're there until one day—whoosh!'

She looked at me coldly, and then she said: 'A one-pound brick of plutonium can give cancer to every man, woman and child on

193

earth.'

I moved away and, sheltering beside a blasted hawthorn tree, tried to light a cigarette. What a place to take a boy camping! My father took me to summery woods, and brewed up while I whittled sticks.

My father lied.

Lesley didn't lie; I had to give her that. Lesley had given our son despair, and the messy breaking-up of a sort of marriage. She hadn't kept her back turned and her voice down; she hadn't told him to hurry out and buy some firelighters.

I shivered in the wind; it was icy. This wasn't a regular stop on our coach schedule. I pictured the brochure. *Come on our Mystery Tour! For that Special 'Day Out with a Difference!' Our Sunday Trip to Greenham Common, where the temperature is always minus zero! Have your Balls Frozen Off while a woman tells you about Nuclear Annihilation!!! Take a Sightseeing Stroll around the Picturesque Dwellings! Watch the Local Craft of Breaking Up Old Boxes to Build a Fire! Pause to Enjoy the Unique Sport of Attempting to Hang Out a Groundsheet in a Brisk East Wind! We wind our way homewards stopping for that welcome Cup of Tea and a Lively Discussion of our Sexual Failures!!!*

*   *   *

Hilda was standing at the fence; a square figure in her tweed coat. She pointed to the wire. From a distance it seemed that a lot of rubbish had blown on to it. She beckoned me, and I came closer. Once I was near I realized my mistake; it wasn't rubbish at all.

'Well fancy that,' she said. 'Perhaps she's left a message.'

Baby clothes were hung up, and toys. A teddy-bear dangled; one of its eyes was missing. Prayers and good luck messages were clipped to the fence; they were sheathed in plastic to protect them from the rain. *'You are beautiful!'* said one. *'The World is Listening,'* said another. *'I'll be Back!'* People had left their addresses: Hamburg, Montreal, Wolverhampton. Nobody seemed to have stayed here for long; they were all somewhere else.

'Oh,' cried Hilda. 'Look at this dear little boy!'

Some children's photos were pinned up: smiling boys and girls, some of them yellowed with age. It reminded me of a cemetery I'd seen in Spain. I felt sick; hung up like that, it seemed that the children must be dead.

Hilda was standing on tiptoe, inspecting them.

'I don't know what he looks like!' I wailed.

'Edward?' She shook her head. 'He's not here. None of them are. They've vanished into thin air.'

*   *   *

We walked back to the coach. I was plunged into gloom. I wished we had never come; it was a stupid idea. I thought of all those children's faces, lifting and falling in the wind.

Hilda sat down, rubbing her hands warm. I fished in the carrier bag and took out the Kendal Mint Cake. I climbed down and went across to the nearest fire, where the American woman was crouched, eating a chocolate biscuit. I gave her the mint cake.

'What's this?' she asked.

'It's specially made for extreme conditions,' I said. 'Mountaineers and Arctic explorers. Just the ticket for here.'

'Wow.'

'Go on, you need it.' I looked around. Now I counted, there weren't many women here at all. 'I'm sorry about the coach.'

'What do you mean?'

'That I hadn't brought anyone with me.'

She shrugged. I made my way back, across the worn grass. How dirty my coach looked, in the sunshine!

*   *   *

We drove back to Reading; it was only twenty miles. Stuffed into the cubbyhole was that pathetic carrier bag, with the rest of his gifts in

196

it. I might as well give the lot away.

'I put the oven on the timer,' said Hilda, looking at her watch. 'Should be browning nicely.'

'What a depressing place.' I turned to her, irritably. 'You could've found out where she was going!'

She went pink. 'I told you! Don't blame me. What could I do? I couldn't even send on her beastly mail!'

I drove on, for a moment. 'What mail?' I asked. 'You said she didn't have any.'

'Hardly any,' she sniffed. 'One or two things.'

'But don't you see? If we open it, we might be able to find out where she's gone.'

'How?'

'There may be a clue.' I turned the corner into her street, and stopped outside Lots o'Fun. 'There may be something.'

*   *   *

The problem was, she couldn't find it. Two or three envelopes had arrived, she said, addressed to Lesley, but it was a year ago and she couldn't remember where she had put them.

'They're somewhere, I'm sure,' she muttered, scrabbling through her desk.

I sat, slumped in the armchair, drinking Triple Strength Export from the can. I felt yobbish and mutinous. What was I going to do with the rest of my life?

'Now, Hilda, where were they?' she twittered, searching through the bookshelves and moving her holiday souvenirs. She had a collection of dolls in national costume; they made me want to cry.

She went into the kitchen; she opened cupboards and lifted the lids from canisters, but she couldn't find the letters.

We had lunch. Afterwards I dozed. Outside it grew dark. Sunday afternoon in Reading—could anything be more depressing? I had reached the moment of truth, the end of the road. There was absolutely nothing left.

I looked at my watch. Six o'clock. I had to get up, thank Hilda, drive to London and pick up the pieces of some sort of life. Tomorrow was Monday. I must return the coach to Reg, get a bollocking, lose my job and start the long, long battle with my wife. Ex-wife. Face the washing-up, face the music, face the future. Stand in the shopping precinct and yell. Drink myself to oblivion. What did blokes in my position do?

'Let's have a waffle!'

I jerked awake. Hilda was standing in the kitchen doorway; she had changed into the dress with the frilly collar.

'A waffle?'

'Just for fun.' She smiled at me, brightly. 'Let's! I haven't used my waffle-maker for

198

yonks.'

I paused. 'I'm not hungry.'

She looked stricken. 'Oh please!'

I suddenly sat up. 'Stuff, stuff, stuff all day long!' I shouted. 'What's that going to solve?'

There was a silence. Her eyes filled with tears. So did mine.

Her shoulders sagged. I jumped up and put my arms around her.

'I'm sorry,' I muttered. I hugged her. Her breasts pressed against me like small puddings; for some reason they surprised me.

'Come on!' I pulled away, and went into the kitchen. 'Let's!'

She blew her nose. Then she showed me how to make the batter. I put on an apron; she passed me the milk and the flour and I put them into the liquidiser.

'Isn't this a hoot!' I chortled.

She was humming, so I started humming too. I hummed *Poetry in Motion*, and then I started singing.

'*Oh-a-tree in motion*,' I sang, pressing the shuddering liquidiser. '*See her gentle sway . . .*'

'That's wrong,' she said.

'What?'

'It's *Poetry in Motion*,' she said.

'You're too young to remember that,' I said gallantly.

She turned her back to me, opened the cupboard and pulled out the waffle-maker. 'As a matter of fact, I'm forty-one.'

I paused. 'Gosh.'

She plugged in the waffle-maker.

I said: 'I didn't mean gosh. I meant—*gosh*.'

'Pour it in here,' she told me, opening the machine.

* * *

It didn't function. We both felt ridiculously upset, I don't know why. It was half-past seven, a stupid time to be making waffles anyway, but by now a waffle seemed the only possible thing to do.

'Bloody object!' she cried. 'Bloody, bloody object!'

We stood back, staring at it. Our fragile good cheer drained away. She kicked the fridge. I changed the fuse in the plug, but it still didn't work. We gazed at what had become a useless lump of metal. I thought of the heaps of broken appliances in Costas's shop; they all waited for me.

'Where's the instructions?' she muttered, and went to a drawer. 'With your guarantees, Hilda.'

She pulled the drawer open, viciously, and rummaged amongst bits of paper. 'Washing machine!' she cried, 'Toaster, electric toothbrush!' She flung out bits of paper. 'Liquidiser, digital clock, iron!' Paper whirled around, like leaves in a gale. 'Hair dryer, typewriter, other beastly electric toothbrush

200

that never worked!' Her voice rose, hysterically. 'Coffee grinder, electric carving knife, Lesley's letters!'

She stopped. I turned, slowly. She lifted out four envelopes and gazed at me. 'I knew they were somewhere safe,' she said, and then we both started laughing.

Letter one: From—*L. Weinstein, LDS, BDS, Dental Surgeon.* Reminding *L.B. Featherstone and E. A. Featherstone* that *Your six-monthly dental examination is now due. Could you please telephone and arrange an appointment.*

Letter two: From—*Reading Public Libraries.* Advising *L. B. Featherstone that 'Forgotten Women in History' (L. Tims) and 'Coping with Depression' (C. Gittings) are now overdue. Please return these books at your earliest convenience.*

Letter three: From—*Ben. To—Edward. I am having a Birthday Party on 16 November, and Hope you can Come! 4.30–6.30. RSVP. P.S.: Come Dressed as an Alien.*

I put those aside and opened the last one: a thick, cream envelope.

Letter four:

Col. and Mrs R.E.P. Featherstone,

The Copse,
South Lane,
Sittingfold,
Glos.
Tel: Sittingfold 372

Darling Lesley,
Much as you dislike 'committing' yourself, I fear
that Christmas is nearly upon us, yet again, and
your father and I would like to finalize
arrangements. Im sure this is very boring of us
but, believe it or not, we also have a life to lead.

Now we come to the tricky part. Much as we
enjoyed your 'therapist' friend's participation in
village life—a lasting memory for many,
especially our vicar—I think we can all agree
that last Christmas was not perhaps our most
successful on record. I wonder if the woman in
question would be happier, this year, to pass the
festive season in the bosom of her own family,
rather than ours? It would also give us a chance
to get to know our own grandchildren, sorely
missed and sorely loved.

Bright today, but cold. Tell Vicky that the
Frost Fairy was busy last night (mostly wreaking
havoc with the last of the chrysanths). Daddy has
painted the attic room for Edward—do be polite
about the colour.

With all my love, darling,
As always,
Mummy.

P. S. I would phone, but you know what happens then.

I laid it on the sink, gazed at Hilda, and let out my breath.

'Well?' said Hilda.

I pointed to the phone number: Sittingfold 372.

'We've got her!' I whispered.

CHAPTER SEVENTEEN

We dialled Lesley's parents all evening, but it wasn't until 11.00 that we got a reply. I had told Hilda to talk to them—her explanation seemed less complicated than my own.

I sat on the settee smoking a cigarette and listening to her speaking. She said that she was Lesley's ex-flatmate and felt like looking her up again, for old times' sake. Silence as she listened, the receiver to her ear. She met my eye and gave me a thumbs-up sign—how precious this dumpy woman was to me! She gestured for a pencil and paper, I gave it to her and she wrote down an address.

Then she said goodbye and replaced the receiver. 'She's living in Deal.'

'Deal?'

'Deal, Kent.' She showed me the address: *14*

Leaps Road, Deal, and a phone number.

'She's there now? You sure?'

Hilda nodded. 'They've been visiting her this weekend. They've only just got home.'

*   *   *

I found the code and dialled the number.

Lesley answered. 'Hello?'

I couldn't speak.

'Hello?' said Lesley. She sounded sleepy. 'Who's there?'

My hand started trembling. I put the receiver down.

Hilda jabbed me in the ribs. 'Cowardy custard!'

*   *   *

I decided to go that night. I shaved, and for some reason brushed my teeth. I had a long session on the toilet, as if my body needed to evacuate itself, in readiness. Hilda ran me a bath and I lay there, deep in foam, with my eyes closed. The warmth seeped into every pore of my skin.

When I was dry I dusted myself all over with her Johnson's Baby Powder. The mirror was steamed up; I moved in a haze. Then I got dressed, carefully, buttoning my shirt to the neck.

I rubbed the mirror and, borrowing her

scissors, cut some stray hairs out of my nostrils and ears. I felt like a virgin, preparing herself for her wedding. I felt I was going on a long voyage, very long, and I didn't know when I would return.

In the lounge, I draped a towel round my shoulders and Hilda cut my hair.

'Nobody's done this since my wife,' I said.

She knew a bit about Eleni but now I told her about my son. Snip-snip went her scissors as I told her the truth—if I knew what the truth was, by now. This past week had buffeted me in so many directions. But I told her about Lesley, and what had happened eleven years before, and how I had been searching all over England for Edward.

She didn't seem surprised. She tilted my head sideways, frowning with concentration, and snipped round my ears.

'Gosh,' she said, 'you've got freckles here too.' Then she added: 'Little business matter, my foot.' She chuckled. 'You've been talking about that boy for two solid days.'

I paused. 'Do I sound a cad?' I asked.

She stopped snipping. 'No,' she said. 'You sound—ever so lonely.'

*   *   *

She was coming with me. I couldn't decide if I was pleased or not. What about her job? Tomorrow was Monday—in fact it was nearly

205

Monday now.

'Bugger my job,' she said, buttoning up her coat. 'Bugger the Gas Board.'

She made us a thermos of coffee; she packed up the flapjacks into a Tupperware box and bound it with stout elastic bands.

'You got a radio?' she asked. 'We've got to keep you awake.'

It was such a relief, to be taken in hand. Why had no woman ever done this before? 'Got any cassettes?' I asked.

'Have I got cassettes? he asks. Of course I've got cassettes.' She went to the shelves and pulled out a handful. 'Come on,' she said, putting them into a carrier bag.

At just past midnight, we slipped out of the flat.

CHAPTER EIGHTEEN

Hilda had brought her knitting. Click-click went her needles; it's a lovely sound. She sat in the front seat, across the aisle.

'I was bored anyway,' she said. 'Stuck in a rut.' She disentangled Ricky Nelson and slotted in a cassette. '*Oklahoma*,' she said. 'I adore show music.'

'My wife said I was stuck in a rut. My music used to drive her round the bend.'

'Bit of a fuddy-duddy, were you?' she asked.

'No! It's just that they don't sing them like they used to.'

'That's what I meant.'

'What?'

'A fuddy-duddy.'

I glared at her. 'Whose side are you on?'

*　　*　　*

We drove along the M4. It was dark and empty. *Oh, What a Beautiful Morning* played. I was glad Hilda was there.

I said: 'I thought we'd have these big Greek get-togethers, me and her family. You know, kebabs and dancing and stuff. But we never did. She liked dancing but not that sort. We never went to Greece either. She preferred Spain. Once we went to these self-catering apartments, near Benidorm, for our holidays. The sort of places where you buy your own Corn Flakes. She started flirting with this bloke called Alan. He used to work-out, and every morning she'd be up bright and early—she never used to get up early at home, you had to crowbar her out of bed—and I'd look down from the balcony and there I'd see her yellow towel, laid out on the lounger next to his, beside the pool. And she suddenly got helpful about the shopping—she usually hated shopping—and she'd offer to go to the supermarket and she'd be away hours. I'd look down and there would be his lounger, empty

207

too, and his blue towel beside it. And then she'd come back and all she'd bought was a packet of tea bags.'

'Anyway, I got to know him and I found out he did TT racing. Well, I'd had a bike too, a Norton, and so we started talking bikes. He'd even gone across America on a Harley Davidson; he was really interesting. So we ended up mates. She lay in the sun and got so huffy, she wouldn't let me rub in her suntan oil. She wouldn't even let *him*. She went off and tried her luck with the barman; but it was Saturday by then and we were leaving Sunday.

'I tried to joke her out of it. We were packing up, the Sunday, and I pointed to all our bits of food we were leaving behind, and I pretended to be our maid's husband, having dinner that evening. "Ole!" I said, "It'sa Sunday again, it'sa baked beans again, it'sa tomato ketchup and a pineapple chunks, o benissimo! All washed down with half a canna Seven Uppa and Palmolive Washing Up Liquido!" She just said: "Don't be so childish."'

I paused. 'I met her on a beach, you see. That's when I fell in love with her.' I looked at my hands on the wheel. 'Sometimes, when we went on holiday, I thought it would be all right. It would be like that first day. She ran across the sand, then. Everything was new. You keep on thinking that something will do the trick. If you paint the lounge, if you have a child, if you go to Toronto.'

'Toronto?'

If. If only I had a son. You sat back and dreamed. *If only* was the way I did it.

I indicated left and we drove round the interchange, joining the M25. It was one o'clock. I changed gear and we cruised along, in the dark. We hadn't seen a car for so long that I felt we were the last two people alive. Everyone else had vanished and our coach was the only moving object in Britain.

'She was so moody—for no reason, honest. I hadn't done anything wrong. She'd sulk for days, then suddenly she'd be all excited and say let's build a sauna, it'll change our lives, we'll be happy then. So I'd send off for the brochures but when they arrived she'd gone off the idea, she'd forgotten all about it, and she said I was so boring, always fiddling with the house, what good did that do?'

'Flapjack?' Hilda rummaged in her carrier bag. She passed me one and I munched it. It was restful, talking to her. It was like talking to an aunt at bedtime, telling her about your day. A long, long day.

'She said I wasn't interested in her dancing, but what can you say about dancing?' I asked. 'You do it, you don't talk about it.'

'You could talk to that chap about bikes.'

'Dancing's different.' I swallowed the rest of the flapjack. 'Anyway, I was supportive. What did she think I was doing, slaving my guts out so she didn't have to go out to work, so she could go to her bleeding classes.' I swept the crumbs off my trousers. 'And meet other people's bleeding husbands?'

We were silent. I stared at the white lines of the road, endlessly swallowed up by my coach wheels. They tickered towards us, at speed.

Hilda said: 'I know why you married a foreign wife.'

'Why?'

'Because you were too lazy to have an English one.'

I paused. 'What?'

She passed me the thermos cap, filled with coffee. 'You didn't have to understand her so much. You could put it down to her Greekness.' She paused. 'You didn't have to talk.'

'We did talk!'

'It's like, in your job, being a coach-driver, you don't have to talk.'

We drove on for a moment in silence. A single car, its lights glaring, passed in the opposite direction. I said: 'All right. I talked, and she talked. But we didn't always meet in the middle.'

'Sounds as if you didn't like each other much.'

I didn't reply. I drained the coffee, and passed the cup back to her. 'We weren't friends,' I said. 'Not really.' I lit a cigarette. With a click, *Oklahoma* finished. 'I've never been friends with a woman. We've never been

210

able to chat in the bathroom and do the crossword together.' I gazed at the motorway, suffused under the arc lights. 'You're the first woman I've met,' I said, 'who's my friend.'

There was a silence. Then she said: 'Thanks a lot!'

*　　　*　　　*

'She wasn't happy,' I said. 'I didn't notice. You don't notice when you're married, there's always so many things to do.' I paused. 'When I went back to my house, last Sunday, it felt different. I told myself it was just tidy, and his things were there, but it was more than that.' I took a breath. 'It felt like a happy home.'

We had finished the flapjacks but we were still on the M25. It seemed to go on forever. This felt like the longest journey I had ever taken. Perhaps it was these dead hours of the night; however fast I drove, time moved so slowly.

'My parents weren't happy,' I said, 'if you want to know the truth. They never had rows, they never raised their voices. But I knew.'

'Sound like mine.'

'I had to make them happy, in my head. I had to think I was like other children.'

'You were like other children,' she said.

'Not all!' I cried. 'Not all!'

'All right. Not all. Coffee?' She refilled the cap and passed it to me.

211

'If they don't love each other, then it's like there's no bottom to the world. Nothing to stand on.'

'So?'

'I used to build these garages for my cars,' I said. 'And these farms for my farm animals. I always loved doing things with my hands. I practically rebuilt the house in Orpington.'

'Then along came the big bad wolf, and blew it all down,' she said. The needles clicked. 'Must've been jolly flimsy to begin with.'

We were silent. 'I'm glad she and I never had any children,' I said. I thought of Edward: had he fared any better? Did he have something to stand on?

*　　　*　　　*

'My mother wanted another child,' I said. 'And when I was three she found she was pregnant again. She was thrilled; my father was thrilled. They wanted a girl this time.' I paused, and lit another cigarette. 'Months passed and it all seemed to be going fine.' I stopped.

They cast this foggy glow, arc-lights; have you noticed? At night, motorways seem mistier, and dimmer. And always the same. You might have travelled one mile or twenty, it doesn't make any difference.

'Well?'

I looked at the little lights in my radio. I didn't speak for a while. Then I thought why not? I took a breath. 'When she was six months pregnant she had a miscarriage. Nobody was there except my father. My mother was in the bathroom. He wrapped this little object in a tea-towel, he couldn't quite bring himself to use newspapers, and then he put that into an old pillowcase, and he took it out to the allotments, out the back.' I paused. 'It was the middle of the night, and nobody saw. He didn't bury her in his allotment because he was worried in case he dug her up again. So he got his spade and dug a hole near the hedge, where they put the rubbish. It took so long, he said, to dig it deep enough, it took hours. And then he put the bundle in.' I stubbed out my cigarette. 'Neither of them ever mentioned it again. He never even told her where he had buried it. Her. My sister.'

I had stopped the coach. We were parked on the hard shoulder. At some point I had switched off the engine. It was dead quiet; the needles didn't click any more.

'They never really touched each other again after that,' I said. 'He was building his garage, and he had his bowls—he was the captain. It's amazing how you need hardly be together at all, if you're married. And then there's the telly.' I spoke to the steering wheel. 'When I was a child I thought all parents had twin beds. Once, he said something to me.'

'What?'

I stopped. 'It doesn't matter.'

'Go on.'

'He said: *"Do you know what the five most chilling words in the English language are?"* I asked what. And he said: *"Pull my nightie down afterwards."*'

There was a silence. *West Side Story* was playing, but I couldn't hear the words. I gazed at the wheel.

'He didn't tell me any of this until he was in hospital. I used to visit him, and that's when he talked. He'd never told me anything before but he knew he was going to die. Ridiculous, really, because by that time he could hardly speak.' I paused, and watched the lights pulse on the radio. 'He had lung cancer.'

A moment passed. The motorway was empty.

Hilda said: 'You poor love.'

She patted the seat beside her. I got up, moved across the aisle and sat next to her. She shifted her knitting and I leant against her. She was too small, so I snuggled down in my seat and leant my cheek against her shoulder. It felt soft and upholstered.

'Don't want to be like him, do you?' she asked.

I shook my head.

She fished inside my anorak pocket and pulled out my packet of cigarettes.

'Like father, like son,' she said.

'I'm not!' I cried. 'Really I'm not.'

She opened the door and threw the

214

cigarette packet out.

'Litterbug, Hilda!' she said to herself.

And they I went back to my seat and we drove on.

*   *   *

That's how I gave up smoking. By two o'clock we had joined the M2, the Dover road. I was back in Kent, where I was born and grew up; where I had lived as a married man. It had pulled me back, as if something hot and alive was drawing in its breath. It felt odd, as if all this time I hadn't really travelled at all. Only my mileometer and my aching back told me I'd been on the road for a week. And there was Hilda, of course, who hadn't existed until this weekend. She was the only person alive who knew about my sister.

They were going to call her Mary, my sister. She would be thirty-nine now, and looking in the mirror for wrinkles. By speaking about her aloud, I suddenly missed her. Of course we would have been friends. She would be that woman who liked doing the crossword. She would have taught me how to live, just as Edward would have taught me. On and off, all these years, I had wondered about her in the same way I had wondered about my son— would she have had freckles, would she have laughed at my jokes? Like Edward, every possibility existed in her.

Edward lay sleeping in Deal. I had made the phone ring in his house. Now I knew he was there, for a certainty, it seemed dangerous for us to meet. Did I even want to?

I needed Hilda, with her knitting, to stop my fear. Or to stop me thinking that it really wouldn't make any difference at all, whether I met him or not.

CHAPTER NINETEEN

It's three o'clock and I'm freewheeling into Deal, my engine switched off. My coach feels as light as kitchen foil. This is my final trip, the Mystery Tour to end all tours. It's a moonlit night and all along the beaches of Southern England people are playing on the sand. I have carried them there—this year, last year, who knows? Senior citizens are dancing silently beside the sea. Their hair is silvered by the moon. They have been dancing all this time because I have forgotten to take them home. Who wants to go home anyway? You go home and there's no home to go to. *Address unknown.* There's a stranger looking out of your window. Where your home used to be, there's empty space.

No wonder the beaches are filled. Some women have set up camp; their plastic tents flap in the wind, like hands attracting my attention. Nothing can be relied on, these women would be saying if only I could hear them. Radios are planted in the sand; they glint like bombs. They must be playing music, from Margate to Hythe to Hastings to Brighton. The foam is lined with young women, prancing like fillies, rows of them tossing their heads. They're neighing for men, they're baying at the moon. They have small breasts and slender hips. Their unborn children fill the beach, jostling for space. Some of them are playing and some of them are half-buried in the sand. One or two, just their heads are showing.

In my coach the cassette is singing; it's something from *West Side Story* but I can't hear it. I'd like to find my parents in this crowd but I know I never brought them here. They're in disgrace. They didn't deserve to come, though I loved them better than anybody in the world. Anyway, they might have brought my sister with them and I'd rather not, just now.

The moon shines on the swollen sea. *What is this thing called love?* Amongst the crowds there are couples, there must be, I'm sure they must be married. I've met so many of them, I've driven across England, my back's aching. If only I could see their faces I might recognize them, but they've all turned away. I don't know what marriage is, any more. Piff might be able to tell me, but when I spot her sitting on the sand she has shrunk into an old woman; when she turns away, her sequined jacket winks.

Behind me, Deal is dark. The town is sleeping, and the only lights come from the telephone kiosks. There's a lot of them; there seems to be one kiosk on each street corner. They are so bright they hurt my eyes.

One of the phones is ringing. I drive soundlessly from one to the other; the ringing always seems to come from the next one, a street further on.

I drive through the town, my ears ringing, and when I get to the last kiosk I know it's this one, I can hear the ringing quite clearly. I run in and lift the receiver.

Edward is on the line; I can hear him breathing.

'Hello,' I say.

Silence.

'Hello?' I raise my voice.

There's no reply.

'Edward?' I say. 'It's me. Dad.'

Still no reply.

I open the door of the kiosk and stand out in the street, holding the receiver in my hand. I shout into the night: 'I've got a son in here!'

There is a silence, then I hear a scratchy sound from the receiver. He is speaking.

I press it to my ear. It's my son's voice and he's talking quite clearly. The trouble is, it's gibberish. The words are all the wrong way round and I can't understand what he's saying.

'Lousards,' he says.

'What?'

'Lousards. Alibaba numsquitchin.'

'Hang on!' I cry. 'Say it again!'

But the line goes dead.

CHAPTER TWENTY

It was three in the morning when we drove into Deal. Hilda was dozing, to the final chorus of *Oliver*. It was a town of the dead. The only illuminations were the street lamps and the empty telephone kiosks. They waited on street corners. One of them was ringing, I was sure it was. I heard it. I would pick it up. All I had to say were two words: *I'm here.*

I drove along the seafront. It was a cold, moonlit night. The beach was empty; it was low tide and I saw the pallor of the sand. The moon, reflected, made the water look swollen and oily.

Hilda grunted and rearranged herself. The cassette clicked off. I cruised along the road, but in all the Bed and Breakfasts the windows were dark. Everybody had gone to bed, long before. There is nothing as desolate as an off-season seaside resort. I'd been here once before, with a party of OAPs, but that was in June and in daylight. They had sat on the beach with their stockings rolled down.

I had to put Hilda to bed. I drove around

219

for a while and finally found a hotel, an expensive one with a colonnaded porch and AA stickers. Behind the door, a light glowed. I rang the bell and a porter shuffled up, muttering like someone in Shakespeare.

It was a twin-bedded room and Hilda settled in obediently. She sleep-walked in her pink nightie, and climbed between the sheets.

'Thanks for the company,' I said.

'Aren't you sleepy?' she mumbled. She said something about a hanky. I fished in my pocket. But then I realized she'd not said that, she'd said something about 'hanky-panky'. Eyes closed, she wagged her finger at me.

I shook my head, reassuring her. 'Of course not,' I said. 'I'm a gent.'

She fell asleep. I touched her shoulder, awkwardly, in its flannel nightie. Then I tiptoed out of the room.

*   *   *

I was wide-awake. I had arrived at last; nothing could steal these hours from me, now I was here but not yet announced. I had a few hours' daydreaming left, and I was not going to smoke.

I drove down to the seafront, switched off my headlights and gazed at the water. I've never understood the moon; blink and it's moved. Since my arrival, an hour before, it had slipped down the sky and shifted to one side.

You could trust the good old sun to rise in the right place at the right time, appearing with its flushed face like a pub regular. The moon was as unpredictable as a woman; try snatching at its reflection and all you'd get were empty hands.

I heard the waves. The lake at Windermere made silly little laps; they had reminded me of my wife. Everything had reminded me of my wife—bottle-tops could remind me of my wife. They had told me that I had loved her but I had never liked her. No wonder I'd felt poorly.

The sea's noise was different. It was so vast that it had no borders; rhythmic sighs but more than that, sounds beyond sound. I thought of all the children sleeping in the town behind me. They breathed in unison, vastly; they sighed and turned.

It was strange—the nearer I got to Edward, the more he dispersed. He became scattered into everybody else's children. It was like moving close to a newspaper photo and finding that, in fact, it was only made up of little dots. When I was young, and noticed this for the first time, I had felt tearful, as if the person in the photo didn't exist at all.

*　　　*　　　*

I crawled around the town at 20 mph, looking for Leaps Road. I knew I would find it sooner or later and I was in no hurry. In the dark, I

221

felt like somebody in one of those videos I had been watching—a cop or a criminal. Finally, at four o'clock, I spotted the sign and turned left into a suburban road.

They were semis; they reminded me of Snetterton Road, Bromley, where I was born, and of Croxley Road, Orpington, where I had failed in my marriage. An ordinary sort of place. All the curtains were closed. Number 14 had a fir tree in its front garden and a battered van parked outside.

My heart quickened, like a hunter's. I had got them.

I backed the coach twenty yards or so, and parked on the opposite side of the road, so the house was in view. I waited.

*   *   *

I did drop off, now and then. At one point, in the darkness, I moved across to what I thought of as Hilda's Seat and stretched out. But at 6.30 I sat up; wide-awake. My head was clear. The sky was rosy; it was going to be a beautiful day.

Oddly enough, it was still only Monday morning. So much had happened since Sunday night; during this past week, time had grown and shrunk like elastic. I was two hours from my son. By 8.30 at the latest that yellow door would open and out he'd walk, scrubbed for school. Lesley might take him in the van—my skin tingled when I thought about their domestic arrangements but from the little I remembered this was unlikely. Like my wife, she hated getting up in the morning—I remembered that distant Lesley, on those few distant mornings, grumbling under the sheets while I got ready for work and wondered whether I dared use her razor. Edward was old enough to go to school alone.

I knew exactly what I was going to do. I was going to saunter up, say hello, and announce myself as a long-lost friend of his mother. We would have a chat on the way to the bus stop; we would take the first tentative steps towards friendship. It would be unfair, for me to reveal myself as his father when he thought he had one already. That would come later. I couldn't think of later, yet.

Birds were singing. I waited, as the minutes crawled by. I slotted in one of Hilda's cassettes and listened to the theme from *A Man and a Woman*. I had seen the film, too, and it vaguely worried me that I couldn't remember who I'd seen it with. *Da da da da-da-da-da-da da da da-da-da.* Perhaps I'd been alone. But surely no man in his right mind would choose such a soppy picture. I must have been with some girl, close beside me but locked into her own impossible dreams. The actress was Anouk Aimée, gorgeous, but I couldn't remember what the bloke was called. I couldn't even remember his face.

At 7.30 a postman appeared at the end of the street. I watched him feeding the doors with letters. Faintly, a dog barked and then was silent.

He crossed the road in front of the coach and glanced up at me. I realized, for the first time, how high-up I must look. The tape had finished and I was sitting in silence, thinking of bacon and eggs. He raised his eyebrows at me and I grinned back. He walked on.

When I looked at the houses again, one or two curtains had been drawn open. Not Lesley's. Behind me I heard the rattle of a milk float. I felt familiar with these houses by now, like you feel familiar with somebody you've slept beside. I'm not talking about sex, mind, but sleep. You've gone through hours of dreams and a change of light. I felt part of this road's waking-up.

Then I thought: my son is more familiar with this milkman and this postman than he is with his own father. What's the world coming to?

By eight several people had left their houses and gone to work.

One bird was still singing, I heard it in the

gaps between the *Oklahoma* songs. I was listening to the tape again. *Oh, what a beautiful morning* . . . In one doorway, not Lesley's, a woman in a dressing gown stood, a child on her hip, waving her husband goodbye. She lifted the child's arm and pumped it up and down, but her husband didn't see.

Lesley's house needed a coat of paint. I wondered if she had rented it; this didn't look like her sort of neighbourhood, but then I didn't really know her any more. I wondered what the crisis had been, in Reading, and why she had suddenly left. I wondered if Barry had visited, to see his daughter. Perhaps he had come home and it wouldn't be my son opening the front door, it would be a bloke as sexy as Elvis Presley.

I switched the tape off, so I could concentrate. The curtains were still closed. Now I was here I felt detached, as if I was suspended a few inches off the ground. I suddenly couldn't believe that anything could happen.

In the next house to Lesley's the door opened and two teenage girls came out, wearing school coats. One had a red scarf wound round her head. They walked away, up the road. I was freezing, from sitting in the same position for so long. My bladder was bursting. I wondered if Lesley was living with somebody else by now. A year had passed; anything could have happened. Why hadn't she left a forwarding address?

At 8.25 a car came down the street. I hadn't noticed it. I only saw it when it stopped outside Lesley's house, double-parked beside the van.

Its horn sounded, briefly, and then, so quickly I hardly glimpsed it, the front door opened and a schoolboy ran out. He jumped into the car, it pulled out and drove away.

*   *   *

Have you ever tried to turn a coach in an average-size street? I started the engine, cursing its three little coughs. Finally I revved it up, in a cloud of exhaust smoke, and drove to the end of the road, keeping the car in my rearview mirror. At the end of the street it turned left, so at the other end of the street I turned right. Fumbling, I engaged the wrong gear and juddered along in third. Luckily the streets were laid out like a grid, so I accelerated down the parallel one, back towards the main road.

Luckily, too, it's steam before sail and the traffic was forced to stop as I swung into the road. There was a squeal of brakes. The car, a blue estate job, was speeding away and there were several vehicles between us. I swore at myself. Why hadn't I guessed that he'd be given a lift?

The traffic lights had changed to red but I put my foot down. Somebody hooted. The car was disappearing round a bend, ahead of me. I was stuck behind a British Telecom van. I pressed the horn.

Glued to its bumper, I drove round the comer. Ahead lay a large intersection; the blue car indicated right and pulled across the road. I drew out, but the Telecom van blocked me and I watched the car, helplessly, as it disappeared behind a derelict church.

The van waited patiently for three cars, a lorry and a bus to pass before it pulled out and crossed the road. I followed, trying to nose my coach past it, cursing my size.

The van indicated left and turned down a side street. Ahead, the road was empty. I drove to the end and stopped at a T junction. To the left, a sign pointed to an Industrial Estate, Units 1–7; to the right there was a street, lined with hoardings, and a boy, bicycling into the distance.

I watched him; he wore a school blazer. I turned his way and drove down the road. The hoardings gave way to a building site; I had to slow down for a bulldozer. Beyond the site was a carpet warehouse, then a Baptist chapel proclaiming JESUS IS WATCHING YOU. I drove past a group of bungalows and jammed on the brakes. Ahead stood a glassy modern building, set back from the road. Children were filing through the gates. Several cars were parked outside, and I was just in time to see the blue estate car, its passengers gone, pull out and drive away.

*   *   *

It was 9.15 when I got back to Leaps Road. This time I parked on the main road; I preferred to be on foot it made me less conspicuous. I was more wary of Lesley than of my son.

I walked up the street towards the house. I simply couldn't think of anything else to do. God knew what I was going to say; there was no point planning when nothing turned out the way I expected anyway. Suddenly I felt exhausted. I'd missed my son, yet again; he'd slipped through my fingers. Now I was here, a few yards from his house, I felt drained. How many houses had I approached, my heart thumping, this past week? Arsenal, Leicester, Windermere, Reading, Spalding. Perhaps, now I knew he was a real boy, I should give it all up and go back to London.

I stopped. On the other side of the street, Lesley's door was opening. A woman came out, holding the hand of a little girl.

I stared at her. I thought: fancy Lesley having an au pair.

She wore a black shiny raincoat and her hair, short as a lavatory brush, was bright orange. I was too far away to see her well. She knelt down and buttoned up the little girl's coat, then they started walking down the street.

However much people change, their walk remains the same. It was Lesley. She had lost weight and dyed her hair, but it was unmistakably her. I ducked down behind a car. She took the girl up the path of a neighbouring house and rang the bell. A woman, holding a baby, opened the door; Lesley kissed her little girl goodbye and left her there.

Before I could move, she went back to her van and climbed in. It took her a while to get it started, I heard the grinding engine noises as I walked quickly away, to the corner of the main road.

By the time the van appeared at the corner I was in my coach. I started the motor, and when the van pulled into the traffic I followed it.

She was still a terrible driver. The van swung out, without indicating, and overtook a car. I thought bitterly: she should never have passed her test. She wasn't fit to be in charge of a van, let alone two children, dragging them across England, in and out of rented accommodation and unsuitable love affairs, therapy and trance-dances, dumping them with child-minders and exposing them to the elements on Greenham Common. Some mother she was. How dare she dispense with fathers so blithely? Now I knew she hadn't taken Barry back I felt a pang of sympathy for him.

229

I followed the van as it weaved its erratic way through the backstreets of Deal. It faltered, then accelerated over a zebra crossing, stopping an old lady in her tracks. At the next traffic lights I caught it up. On its back window were two stickers. One said GIVE BLOOD and the other said STOP ACID RAIN. Typical, I thought: the bossy tone, the self-righteousness. It reminded me of her demand to Save the Trees while she was busy stealing my son. What could I do about blooming Acid Rain? It was so female, to make other people feel vaguely guilty all the time, like seasickness.

By the time the van stopped I had worked myself up to boiling point. I drew in, further down the street, and turned to watch her.

It was a back street, with a short parade of shops. She opened the back of the van and took out a packing case, which she carried across the road. Then she put it down and unlocked the door of a shop. It was called *The Treasure Trove*. She took the packing case in, then a moment later she reappeared and put out some boxes on the pavement. They looked like old records. She changed the sign to OPEN and went back inside the shop.

I switched off the engine and climbed out.

CHAPTER TWENTY-ONE

'How much for the Bo Diddley?' I asked cheerily, holding up the record.

She was sorting out the packing case. '50p,' she said, 'if it was outside.' She straightened up and turned. She paused, then she said: 'I'm not really open yet.'

There was a silence. I was still standing beside the door.

She looked at me and frowned. 'Christ,' she said. 'It's you.'

I nodded. 'Yep. It's me.'

It suited her, to be thinner. Her face didn't look exactly older, so much as weathered. She looked more interesting than her squarer, younger self—more lived-in. She would never be beautiful. Her orange hair stood up stiffly; it made her look more startled than she sounded.

'Just passing by,' I said. 'Thought I'd say hello.' I had to be genial; I had to tread carefully.

'How did you know I was here?'

I shrugged. 'I 'ave my methods,' I said. 'I verk for Reading Public Libraries.'

'What?'

'You 'ave two of our books.'

She sat down, heavily, at one of the tables.

'You don't look any older,' she said.

'Really?'

'You look exactly the same.'

I didn't know how to take this; I couldn't pretend she'd said it with any warmth.

She lit a cigarette. It was a small shop, crammed with junk—coal scuttles, old photos, that sort of thing. It smelt like a suitcase does, when you haven't used it for years and you've finally got the lid open.

'You haven't, by any chance, got a cup of tea?' I asked lightly.

She got up and put on the kettle. I sat down on a wobbly chair; it was too small for me.

'Fancy you running a shop!' I said.

'Why shouldn't I?' she snapped.

'Nothing. I mean, well . . .'

'It's my own place, I'm doing something for myself, at last.'

'What about, you know, the sociology and everything?'

'Read the government figures?'

I nodded.

'Well, then.'

She turned away. I looked at her back. She was wearing baggy red trousers. With the orange hair it gave her an unlikely, clownish air. I thought: this woman is the mother of my son.

I realized I hadn't read a newspaper for a week. It was as if I had been locked away in an institution, or sent on some obscure holiday. I felt odd, sitting there. My mind was still, dreamily, with my earlier possibilities, back in Windermere and Spalding. I couldn't catch up with myself and what was happening. My bones felt numb, on the hard wicker chair. She was familiar enough with me to be abrupt, and yet it wasn't quite personal enough to be directed at me, Desmond. I craved one of her cigarettes; she owed me about a hundred, but it seemed tactless to remind her.

'You want it ordinary, I suppose?' she asked.

'Ordinary?'

'I've got camomile and ginseng and—'

'Aaargh!' I clutched my throat.

She opened a caddy. 'Still teaching people to drive?'

'No. I work for a coach company now.'

There was a silence. We seemed like two strangers, but more wary. Two unknowns, but without that small store of goodwill you keep for somebody you've just met. I looked at her trousers and tried to remember her stout thighs wrapped around me, but it was as if it had never happened. This was depressing. Yet an eleven-year-old boy sat in a classroom, this very morning, just a mile away. The room was so stuffy; its objects seemed to clamour at me from the walls. I felt dizzy. I scratched my nose; it felt rubbery, as if it belonged to someone else.

'I don't suppose you've come to see me.'

'Why not?' I yelped.

233

'You've had sleepless nights, thinking about me.'

I paused.

'At least you've always been honest, unlike some people I know.' She sighed. The kettle steamed, and clicked off. 'You were too masculine to be devious.'

'Thanks,' I said doubtfully.

She brought a cup of tea to the table. I wished she had made one for herself.

She said: 'You can't see him.'

'I didn't—'

'You've come to see Edward.'

'Not really. I just—'

'You can't, Desmond.'

I stood up, and beckoned her to the window. She moved nearer, reluctantly. I pointed through the glass.

'See that?'

I pointed to the rear view of my coach. It looked large and dirty; it filled the street.

'I'm on my way to Dover to collect some holiday-makers,' I said. 'I'm only staying for five minutes.'

Me, devious?

She relaxed, a little, and stubbed out her cigarette on the top of a pile of old saucers. 'You got kids?' she asked.

I shook my head.

She sat down. 'He's a smashing boy. He's been really supportive.'

Supportive? Children shouldn't have to

be supportive, surely. That was the parents' job. I didn't say anything. I had to play her, delicately, on a string. It was touch and go.

'He's kept me going, him and Vicky,' she said. 'Stopped me going under.'

'They make sense of it all, don't they?'

I stopped; I hadn't meant to say that. She looked at me sharply. I drank some tea.

'Does he know who his real father is?' I asked.

She pulled out some newspaper bundles from the packing case and started unwrapping a wine glass. 'He thought another bloke was for a while, a bloke I lived with, but when he buggered off I told Edward the truth. I didn't want him to think that men just dumped their children.'

They don't! I wanted to shout.

'That they were such sods,' she said.

Fuck 'em and forget 'em: that's what men were supposed to do. Nowadays, women seemed to have joined in. Sitting there, I suddenly remembered how I'd felt that day in the Wimpy Bar, eleven years before, when she had told me. I'd felt like women must feel; I'd felt used.

'Some role model this bloke made,' she said, unpacking a sherry decanter. 'Barry. Sitting around waiting for his tea. Getting wrecked every night. Jumping everything that moved.'

I thought of Reg and the unfairness of it all. Reg had four beautiful children who worshipped him; they would be his for life. I watched her as she unwrapped a potty; it was made of cracked china. 'Does he know who I am?'

She shook her head. 'I said it was just a bloke.'

'I'm not just a bloke!'

'I'm sorry,' she said. 'Got a splitting headache. Vicky was up all night.'

I was up all night, I wanted to say. My head throbs too. There was a silence.

'How's he doing at school?' I asked.

'Fine.'

Another silence. 'What's his best subjects?'

'Football and computers.'

She pulled some newspaper off a barometer and propped it up. My parents had had a barometer like that, hanging in the hall. I didn't know how to start or what to say. I sat there on my flimsy chair; any moment it might collapse under my weight. Eleven years of his growing-up, and there was nothing we could talk about. Despite the shorn hair and the changes of address she hadn't altered, it was the same old Lesley, just as I'd dreaded. This past week I'd felt moments of warmth towards her, but it was all wiped out now. Here she squatted, amongst the débris of other people's lives; it seemed so pitiful, life seemed one long chain of breaking-up and scattering, my junk piled up in the garden, Costas's toasters, you grabbed at something and it fell to bits in your hands. My son had slipped through my fingers. I could hear her voice.

'You can't see him, Desmond.'

'He has a right,' I said. 'He has a right to me! He'll want to know.'

'That's his business, when he's old enough.' She glared at me. 'He's just settling down, he's just got used to his new school, you can't come barging in here.' Her voice rose. 'You can't come barging in here, just because you suddenly feel like it! Have you thought about him, what he'd feel?'

'I think about him all the time.'

She looked at me sharply.

'Some of the time,' I said. 'Sometimes.'

'Men, you make me bloody sick. Who's brought him up all these years, who's looked after him, you've never had kids, you've no idea what it's like, trying to earn a living and have some sort of life to yourself, then feeling guilty, always feeling guilty, and split in half, split into pieces, trying to be a mother, it's the hardest bloody job on earth, bringing them up in this terrible world—'

'Why did you have him then?'

'Then you come barging in now all the really exhausting stuff's over, the nappies and the sleepless nights and the measles and asthma and pushing him to playgroup in the pouring rain, and now he's a nice big boy of eleven who doesn't shit in his pants any more here you are, you suddenly decide to miss

237

000him, typical bloody male, all soppiness and sentimentality and let's play train sets together, here you come,' she indicated the window, 'you and your phallic symbol, barging into our lives which are perfectly happy thank you!'

'It's not a phallic symbol!' I bellowed. 'My wife nicked my car!'

I sat there, limp. I was damp with sweat. She sat on the floor. Her face, flushed under its orange tufts, was still talking.

'Men!' she said. 'You're all so cymron and addebabas, you're conglatomy amphidoxed, all my life you've lambammed and simplifixed, you think you're clancymated but you're just jimijinxed.' Her mouth opened and closed. 'Hennanigged,' it said, 'invade and annex, aggrestificate and desficate, and all the time you're hammamamming!'

My head spun. I stood up; my chair rocked.

'Got to get to Dover,' I said.

*   *   *

I parked on the seafront. It was a grey day and the tide was going out; I could tell by the wet sand at the water's edge. I couldn't get out of my seat. I felt as if I'd been punched all over my body; if I moved, my legs would buckle.

Above me, gulls mewled. I could hear them over the traffic. Down on the beach a man was jogging. He was wearing a red tracksuit and

238

when he reached the breakwater he took it in his stride, jumping it like a steeplechaser, and disappeared.

My meeting with Lesley, I had to admit, had not been an unqualified success. How could she have shouted at me like that? What had I done to deserve such an outburst?

I tried to catch up with myself, to visualize her stuffy little shop and to remember what she had said and how I could have replied. It was no good; my mind was numb. I looked down at my carrier bag of gifts; it stuck out, like a tongue, from the cubbyhole. I was stupid to think I'd get anywhere. All I'd got, after a week's driving, was a Bo Diddley record that I realized I'd got on an LP anyway. One of my undamaged LPs, as it happened.

I didn't know what I wanted, but then nobody else seemed to know either. Everywhere I went I was misunderstood. Eric thought I was a dirty bugger, Lesley thought I was a male oppressor, that woman thought I was a child molester, Hilda thought—I didn't know quite what she thought but it made me feel uneasy. The only person who hadn't misunderstood me was my son, but then he'd never met me, had he?

I drove back to the hotel. Hilda must be annoyed by now. But when I got there they said Miss Tucker had gone out. I felt absurdly disappointed. I wanted to sit beside her, like I'd sat in the coach, and lay my head on her

239

shoulder. I'd tell her about Lesley and she'd say: 'Silly billy.' She wouldn't think I was mad, to want to speak to my own son.

It was midday. I couldn't think what else to do, so I phoned the estate agents in Orpington. The girl replied, yes, there was a house just come on the market in Croxley Road. Three bedrooms, front and rear gardens.

She told me the price and added: 'It's been renovated with great care, you see. Fitted kitchen, to the highest standards, and a really super luxury bathroom.'

I nodded in agreement. Then I put down the receiver.

I went to a pub near the seafront, drank a double scotch and ate a plate of Irish stew. That was that, then. *No home today*, warbled the juke box.

At 1.15 I climbed back into my coach and drove to the school.

CHAPTER TWENTY-TWO

I pulled up in front of the gates. I didn't fancy being called a pervert, so I stayed in my coach. I had no plans; I just couldn't think where else to sit, or what to do. I longed for a smoke; the pub had been purgatory.

There was nobody around. The school was

set back from the road and at first it all looked quiet. The playground must be behind the building. A solitary car passed. I looked at my watch; it was two o'clock. They had probably gone back to their lessons, anyway.

Then I saw a man emerge from the school and march briskly towards the gates. He wore a tracksuit. As he came closer he looked at his watch, and quickened his pace. I watched him idly. He opened the gates; he had a whistle round his neck and to my surprise he came up to me and tapped on the window. I got up and opened the door.

'What time do you call this?' He looked at his watch again. His face was red and he was breathing heavily. 'I can't come with you, I've got to take Mr Slatterly in the car.' He turned away and bellowed: 'Boys!'

I looked beyond him, back towards the school. A crowd of boys in football gear was coming towards us.

'*Boys*!' he bellowed again.

The boys broke into a run. They came through the gates and before I could speak they started climbing into the coach.

He said to me: 'See you at the field.' Then he turned away and hurried back towards the school.

The boys were jostling and giggling. 'Sod off, Eddie,' said one, quite distinctly, as they made their way to their seats.

I froze. They clambered past me, chattering.

241

I sat still, holding my breath. I caught various names. Someone else, I was sure, called out: 'Ted! Over here!'

I didn't dare turn round. I inspected them in the mirror. About thirty boys sat there.

I leaned across the aisle and asked the nearest boy: 'What class are you?'

'2b.'

I paused. 'Yes, but how old does that make you?'

He gave me a superior look. 'Nearly twelve,' he said.

I hesitated, but only for a moment. Then I switched on the engine, revved up and pulled out into the road.

*　　　*　　　*

Edward was in my coach. What did they call him—Eddie? Ted? If only I had caught a glimpse of his face this morning, but it had all been too quick.

My heart was hammering; it had moved up my throat. When I tried to change into third, the gears crashed. I pushed the gear stick again; my hands were shaking.

I drove along the road, past the bungalows and the sign saying JESUS IS WATCHING YOU. I could hardly breathe; I was gripped with a reckless exhilaration, as if I'd just led a prison break-out. One of these boys was my son; I had him at last.

I stopped at the intersection and sneaked another look in the mirror. They all wore purple football shirts; they were giggling and chattering. Some of them jumped up and swopped seats. They looked ridiculously similar.

At the intersection I turned right and put my foot down, driving out of Deal. If this was the wrong way to the games field, none of them had noticed yet. People don't, for ages; once they're sitting in a coach they turn into passengers and presume the driver knows where he's going.

The road split into a dual carriageway; I crashed the gears into fourth and we roared along at 60 mph. One of the boys whooped. The sun came out and I had an absurd urge to burst into hysterical laughter, or song. I wanted to bellow at the top of my lungs.

At the next signpost I jammed on the brakes and swerved off to the left. Another whoop. We passed the last few houses and soon we were speeding along beside open fields, heading straight towards the low winter sun. It blazed in the windscreen. With my trembling hand I shaded my eyes. I thought: all this time I've been picturing one little boy, sitting in my coach. Now I've got thirty of the buggers. I juddered with silent, horrified laughter. Which one should I choose? What was the difference anyway?

'Drat it,' said a voice in the seat behind, 'left

me condoms at home.'

Somebody sniggered. Then another voice piped up: 'One drug addict says to the other, can I borrow your needle? No, 'cos you might catch AIDS. It's all right, he says, I've got a condom on.'

I steadied my hands on the wheel. A hot flush rose up my neck. I heard them sniggering; the joke was being repeated, down the coach. There was a far guffaw. Ahead of me, through the filthy windscreen, the sun winked.

I drove on, keeping my eyes on the road. I told myself I hadn't heard what they had said, they weren't really like that. Christ, they were only eleven years old. I felt sick.

'Intercourse,' I heard quite distinctly. Or something like that.

One boy called: 'Pass it here!'

Then another voice shouted: 'Tickler! Tickler!'

The road blurred; my eyes filled with tears. I jammed on the brakes and slewed to a stop beside the road. I switched off the engine, got to my feet and bellowed to them.

'Shut up! *Shut UP!*'

A hush fell. They stared at me.

'Condoms!' I yelled. 'Ticklers! You shouldn't know what a tickler is! It's . . . it's . . .' My voice broke. 'It's too sad!'

A boy stood up. 'Yes sir?' he asked.

I stared. 'What?'

He looked confused. Then the boy beside me, in the aisle seat, pointed to him and whispered: 'That's Tickler.'

There was a silence. 'Tickler?' I asked.

'His name.'

I paused. 'His name?'

'It's Featherstone,' he explained. That's why.'

I stood still, looking down the coach, and stared at my son.

*   *   *

Quickly I turned away and sat down. I drove on. The coach was quiet. Ahead I glimpsed the sea, a silver thread; it glinted in the sun.

The boy in the aisle seat cleared his throat and said: 'Excuse me, mister, but this isn't the way to games.'

I slowed down, at a T-junction, and turned right. We were on the seafront road. There were just a few bungalows here, to one side. To the other was some rough grass, sand dunes really, and then the beach. I stopped the coach; the brakes squealed.

'Let's have games here!' I called. 'Let's!'

A stunned silence, then a whoop. The boys jumped up and fought their way to the front of the coach. I reached under my seat and pulled out the football. I'd jammed it there, days before; it had been sending me mad, rolling about.

Edward was squeezing past, to get to the door. I stopped him.

'Here, Tickler old chap,' I said, and gave him the ball.

He grinned. I glanced at him, casually. He had a square, cheerful face and was covered in freckles—even more freckles than me. At first sight, and I didn't dare look long, I couldn't really recognize myself there. His hair was darker than mine had been at his age. Nearly as dark as Lesley's.

He took the ball and ran across the grass with the others.

*   *   *

The wind whipped my face and the boys leaped and gambolled. Up in the sky the gulls were tossed to and fro, calling to each other. The boys shrieked with laughter; happiness swept over me. I tore off my anorak and flung it onto the ground. I lunged after the ball. We were breaking all the rules, charging each other like bullocks. The blood rushed through my middle-aged veins, I was eleven again, I was yelling raucously. We kicked the ball through the foam, it flew up into the air, the spray arching from it, sparkling in the sun. My face was damp and salty.

A boy flung himself at my ankles and felled me, heavily; they were stronger than I'd expected, these chaps. I was covered in sand; it was in my mouth and my hair. Tears of laughter were streaming down my cheeks. Somewhere the headmaster waited, the grown-ups waited, retribution was at hand. Women were waiting to blame me. They wagged their fingers: do this, do that, don't do any of it, Don't Play On The Grass. Who cared? I'd nothing to lose anyway; no house, no car—no kids, not really, because I was one of them now, just for the heck of it.

Some of them had pulled off their football boots and they were dancing at the water's edge. A hundred miles down this coast, a hundred years ago, Eleni did that, prancing like a filly, and I thought I could never be so happy again. These were all my boys now; they were all the boys I'd ever wanted. They were wrestling on the sand. The wide, empty beach was full of boys, all dressed in purple and all looking the same. One of them was me and we were multiplied until I was dizzy.

I was puffing and panting; I was out of condition. For a week I'd been sitting in a driver's seat. I flopped down on the sand and lay flat out, gazing at the spinning clouds. Edward flopped down, a yard away. He was panting too.

* * *

'You okay?' I asked, sitting up.
He nodded. 'Think so.' He paused for a

247

moment, catching his breath. 'Haven't brought my puffer.'

'It's getting better, the asthma?'

He nodded again. 'Seems to be. Don't know why.'

'It happens. You grow out of it.'

'Do you?'

I nodded.

I looked at him. His nose was blunt, like mine. I could see a resemblance now. Inside me, something shifted. He'd be tall, too; he wasn't stocky like his mother. He had a terrific smile—cheeky. On his chin were two tiny pimples.

His knees were sandy and his feet were bare. I scooped up some sand, it was clammy and cold, and heaped it over his feet. His toes wiggled. He squirmed, giggling. I'd done this before, but I couldn't remember when. Had I dreamed it, or was I dreaming now? I hoped I was dreaming because sooner or later I'd have to take these boys back and face God knew what—the teachers, the police. Perhaps they'd think I was mentally disturbed and lock me up. But if I was dreaming I could simply wake up and find myself in bed.

Which bed? I hadn't got one any more.

I grinned at Edward. 'Got you.' His feet were two lumps; when he shifted, the sand cracked.

He grinned back. 'Want a bet?'

He kicked off the sand and sat, hugging his

knees. He rested his chin on his sandy knees and gazed at the sea. His eyes were grey.

'You like cars?' I asked.

He nodded. 'Mum lets me steer our van, when nobody's looking.'

'I had Dinky cars.'

'Got a remote-controlled Rover, it's wik. But my little sister bust it.'

'Sisters!' I groaned in sympathy. I don't know why, seeing as I hadn't got one.

He pushed the sand around with his toe. His feet were pink with cold; they were surprisingly large. I watched him stirring the sand.

'You like your school?' I asked.

He shrugged. 'It's okay.'

We sat in silence. Far away I heard the cries of the boys, or perhaps it was the gulls. The breeze blew his hair. He had such thin, freckly arms; they were goose-pimpled with cold.

'What's your favourite comic?' I asked.

'*Smash Hits.*'

'*Smash Hits*?' I paused. 'What about, oh, *Beezer* and *Dandy*?'

'They're for babies.'

Then he jumped up and joined the others.

* * *

I parked down the road, out of sight of the school, and told them to be quick. Giggling, they clambered down from the coach. To my surprise, it was still only 3.15.

249

'That was synchical!' one of them said to me.

'What's that mean?' I asked.

'Wik.'

Instead of mud, they were covered with sand. Their white shorts were streaked ochre. I watched them trot briskly up the road and disappear through the gates.

Edward was one of the last to leave. I gave him the football. He hesitated. 'Go on,' I said. 'I don't need it.'

He grinned, and took it.

CHAPTER TWENTY-THREE

I parked outside the hotel and sat in the coach for a moment, brushing the sand off my trousers. I turned. Now the boys were gone I could hardly believe they'd been here. But the seats were sandy and somebody had forgotten his sock; it lay there on the floor, looking chewed. The inside of my coach seemed enormous.

I felt blank. I couldn't catch up with myself. I told myself what had happened: I've found my son at last. I've talked to him and he's talked back. I've buried his feet.

When I went into the hotel they told me Miss Tucker had gone out again, but had left me a note. The manager asked if we were staying another night. I jumped, as if I'd been caught. A normal day was still going on; people were still sitting in offices. I wondered what was happening at the school, and my neck felt hot.

'We'll stay,' I said, simply because I couldn't think where else I'd be.

The note said: *Dear Desmond, Where are you, naughty boy? I've gone to Lesley's house. Love Hilda X.*

*   *   *

I drew up outside Lesley's house, this time in full view of her windows. I felt oddly serene, as if I were a room and somebody had cleaned me out and thrown away the clutter. Perhaps a prisoner feels like this, when he's finally been caught and is going up to trial. All the muddle is over; now he is in other people's hands and there is nothing else he can do.

I switched off the engine and remembered that day at the seaside years before, when I'd fallen in love with my wife. Nothing could take that away from me; she was powerless to spoil it. I'd realized that, today. This afternoon I'd played football on the beach; I'd had my son to myself, for one hour. None of Lesley's shouting could rub that out.

They were in the kitchen. Hilda was drinking a cup of tea and Lesley was drinking a glass of port. The little girl was in the other room watching TV.

Lesley said: 'I went to the school. I thought you'd abduct him.'

I shook my head. 'But they said he'd gone to games as usual,' she said.

'I could have stolen him,' I said. 'It's taken me a week to find you and you weren't even trying to hide. Think how far I could get, if I put my mind to it.'

'What's this sand?' asked Hilda. She brushed down my anorak, making little clicking noises with her tongue. I took it off and she carried it to the back door and shook it out. 'Silly billy,' she said. Outside, through the garden trees, the sky was pink.

'Tea or this?' asked Lesley.

'This,' I replied, and she poured me a glass of port. 'You can trust me,' I said. 'Honest.'

'Can I?'

I nodded. 'I come with a written guarantee.'

'But can you make waffles?' asked Hilda.

'I find it hard to trust people any more,' said Lesley, lighting a cigarette.

'I've been through a bit too,' I said. 'We're in the same boat by now.'

She looked doubtful, and gazed down at her stubby fingers.

'We've been having a nice chat about old times,' said Hilda. She turned to Lesley. 'Remember when we tried to make that zabaglione?'

Lesley smiled, slightly.

Hilda turned to me. 'I've tried to explain things to her.'

'Thank you,' I said.

There was a silence. Lesley refilled my glass.

'What about the shop?' I asked.

'I closed it early.'

From the other room came a jabbering cartoon voice, like a record speeded up, and then the *Popeye* tune. After all these years, children were still watching *Popeye*. Hilda went off to give the little girl her tea.

I didn't know where to begin.

'Why did you leave Reading?' I asked.

'You really want to know?'

'I don't know anything,' I said. 'Anything'll do.'

She paused, and ran her finger round the rim of her glass. 'I had this thing with my therapist,' she said. 'It's the most dangerous thing to do, the most stupid, but when it comes down to sex I seem to get into a bit of mess. She manipulated me, Desmond, she was a very powerful person. She didn't just have my body. She had it all.' She tapped her shorn head. 'All this, in here. All my life I've tried to be independent but she had access to the lot, and Christ didn't she use it.' She paused. 'Why am I telling you all this? You won't understand.'

'I do, honest,' I said. 'I've been married.' I paused. 'Trouble was, my wife didn't want anything inside my head at all.'

'I was incredibly vulnerable,' she said. 'The

253

depressing thing was, she was into all those old power games, the jealousy thing, everything. Just using a different vocabulary. You don't believe it at the beginning, when you're sort of blinded.'

'No,' I agreed. 'Not then.'

'She lived with this other woman and she played us off against each other. I'd trusted her, I'd even taken her to see my parents, like she was my bloody fiancée or something.'

'For Christmas?' I asked.

She nodded. 'Hilda hadn't a clue. She's really straight, she would've been so shocked, you know. She couldn't have handled it.' She inspected a non-existent nail, and chewed it. 'Anyway, this woman, she was going to Greenham Common so I just packed up and went too. Took the kids and everything. And I realized, I was sitting in the bender and it hit me, I realized, Lesley, it's the same old story. I'd come here because of someone else. I think I'm in charge, I'm handling my own life, and it all comes down to bloody sex.'

I nodded. 'It's got a lot to answer for, hasn't it? Sex.'

'I'd meant to go to Greenham for years but I hadn't, had I, I had to wait till I fell in love, like some female in some brainless bloody romance, the sort Hilda reads, the sort I'd sneered at. Some brainless female being swept off her feet. There's nothing left, I thought, nothing left of me, *me*.' She tapped her head

254

again. 'I'd lived with this bloke before, and it was just the same, I'd been sort of emptied, I'd become his property, he'd taken me over, except this time it wasn't stock car racing and listening to stupid jokes, it was different. But exactly the same.' She paused, and chewed on her thumb. 'All these years I'd been aggressive just because, inside, I was weak. I was fighting because I was still incomplete. I knew I could be taken over by anybody.'

Even me? I wondered doubtfully. Was that why she had been so cruel?

She went on. Her voice was flat; she didn't seem to be talking to me, Desmond, but to some interviewer who happened to have arrived at the right, exhausted moment. Perhaps she felt like me—simply too tired to move away again, like a coach that has run out of petrol. At least she'd found out that women could louse her up, as much as men.

'I had my fortieth birthday at Greenham,' she said, 'and I made a decision. I'd keep it to myself—I'd keep that one thing separate. It sounds daft, but it gave me some self-respect. Edward knew, but nobody else. So we made a card, to me, and pinned it on the fence, and nobody ever knew. Just the sky. I told myself: I'm not gay, I'm not straight, I'm not defined by other people. I'm just me. Lesley.' She poured out some more port for herself; she had forgotten about me.

I'd never had time to think about myself like

255

this; I'd been too busy mending the car and trying to please my wife.

'It was a turning point,' she said. 'A fortieth birthday is very important. It gave me the strength to break with her, to break with my old self. I cut myself off from Reading, just like that. I met a woman whose parents were retiring to Portugal and wanted to rent their house, this place, so I came here and started up a whole new life. Celibate.'

I nodded. I was celibate too, now I thought about it. If celibate meant a vast tiredness with the whole business and a disinclination to ever think about it again. I thought of the different routes Lesley and I had taken, these past eleven years, to get here, feeling vaguely mutual, sitting at a table drinking Sainsbury's Fine Old Ruby Red.

It was all too much of a mystery, I couldn't fathom it. Just now, I didn't have the energy. But somewhere en route, along this journey— an even stranger journey than my trip this past week—at some point my son had come into the world, and her daughter, and that was the most mysterious, and yet the most normal, thing of all.

*　　　*　　　*

Outside there was a crackle, and a flash of light.

'They're starting early,' she said.

256

Hilda came into the kitchen. 'See that?' she asked.

'It's November the Fifth!' I cried.

'One Guy Fawkes' night,' said Lesley, 'Barry went out to buy fireworks. The kids and I waited and waited. We'd got everything set up.' She lit another cigarette. 'But he didn't come back till the next morning.'

*　　　*　　　*

Just then, there was a sound in the hall. I froze. Lesley got up and left the room.

I heard Edward's voice: 'Mum, it was weird! This man came to take us to games but he didn't, he took us to the beach—'

Edward came into the kitchen. He put down his schoolbag, and the football, and stared at me.

I grinned. 'Was there a stink?'

'Nobody knew who he was! Who *you* were.' He gazed at me, round-eyed. 'They had this man in from the coach place, and they kept asking him questions. They were ever so angry.'

I chuckled, and Edward started laughing too. Just for a moment I felt I was somebody significant. Perhaps, in a small way, I would always be. In years to come, boys would talk about me with bated breath and wide eyes, as if I was a mythological figure. Something even their Dads could never match. The Superman

257

of Deal; the Phantom Coach Driver. It was probably the only mysterious thing I'd ever done in my life.

Then he saw Hilda and flung himself into her arms.

'Aunty Bun,' he mumbled, buried in her chest. I realized, with surprise, that he was as tall as she was.

Hilda untangled herself and fished out a paper bag. 'Didn't have time to make any, but I found a shop.'

He took something out of the bag. 'Chocolate shortbread,' he breathed.

'The chocolate's not thick enough,' she said knowledgeably. 'But then it never is, when it's bought.'

He munched in silence, his eyes closed. His shoes were tied with multicoloured laces. On his blazer he wore a badge saying *Give a Gnurg a Home*. The three of us sat there, gazing at him.

Vicky came in and installed herself on Hilda's knee. I said: 'What about these fireworks then?'

'Where are they, Mum?' demanded Edward.

'I was going to buy some when I closed the shop, but I forgot.'

'Spasmo-brain!' he said.

'What's spasmo-brain?' I asked.

Lesley got up and tipped her ashtray into the bin. 'Something mothers are.' With her boot, she tried to squash down the content of the bin; it was as overflowing as mine, back in London.

I stood up. 'I'll get them.' I turned to Edward. 'Coming?'

'Are we going in the coach?'

I nodded. He pocketed some more shortbread and rushed out. We heard the front door bang.

I turned to Lesley. 'See you tomorrow, then.'

She froze. Then she actually smiled.

*　　　*　　　*

I put on my anorak.

'Christ,' she said. 'You've joined the CND.'

'People can change,' I said. 'I've even stopped smoking.'

She raised her eyebrows. Then she said: 'Remember some sparklers.'

Just for a moment, we sounded like a proper family.

*　　　*　　　*

The air was clear and frosty. Even in this suburban street there was the tang of the sea. Behind the rooftops a rocket shot into the sky and exploded in glitter. Edward and I climbed into the coach.

'Haven't had fireworks for yonks,' I said.

'My Dad used to do one or two, for me, but it wasn't much fun.'

'Why?'

'He said they were dangerous. He didn't understand that that was the point.'

'It was fun today.'

I nodded, and started up the engine.

I glanced down at the cubbyhole but it didn't seem appropriate, somehow, to give him the presents. By now that other boy, who had never existed anyway, had dissolved and he had taken Sinbad and Mr Toad with him. It wasn't quite that Edward was too old for the gifts, though this might have been the case. It was simply that they were no longer for this Edward. They seemed date-expired.

He showed me where to go—a large newsagent's near the centre of town. It was just closing. A father came out of the door; he had two children with him and their breath smoked in the evening air. Edward and I took his place at the counter, inspecting the depleted display. Just for this evening I was another father, home rather late, with another son. I bought two boxes—the most expensive ones. Perhaps fathers who were late always bought the most expensive boxes.

Then I thought: why should I feel guilty? None of this had been my fault, not really. It was simpler to blame Lesley and call myself a casualty of women's lib. Edward carried out the package; we'd remembered the sparklers.

But I knew that it wasn't this simple. Nothing was as simple as I had thought it; not now. In the streetlight the coach looked as huge as an opera house; some of its curtains were still closed, which gave it a secretive air, as if lives were led in there rather than just journeys taken.

I would miss it, when I gave it back. An old woman stopped and gazed as we climbed in. Suddenly life seemed so strange, and yet so ordinary, that I felt emptied of breath.

I started the engine. 'I drive children to pantos in these,' I said. 'You like pantomimes?'

'Mum took me to *Cats*.'

'Did you like it?'

'Uh-huh.'

'She took you to London?'

'Uh-huh.'

'Just think,' I said. 'We could have met.'

'In Spalding, one of the Ugly Sisters was my teacher. He looked a wally, with his moustache.'

'Would you like to live in London?' I asked. 'See the shows?'

He shrugged. We drove on in silence. Now we were together, I didn't know what we could chat about. I wasn't used to talking to children.

Edward said: 'A boy in my class, his Dad's an actor. He's in the Cup A Soup ad.'

'Fancy that.'

'He's gone to live in Los Angeles now.'

'The boy in your class?'

He shook his head. 'Just his Dad.'

'Ah.' I slowed down and turned into a side road. 'Want to steer?'

'Can I?'

'It's heavy, but you look a big strong boy.' I moved up. 'Squash in.'

He moved across the aisle and sat beside me. 'Wow.' His breath smelt of chocolate.

We crawled along. I kept my fingers lightly on the lower rim of the wheel, to steady it. He leant forward—he had to stretch across the gap—and gripped the wheel. Now it was happening, I felt like some other father with somebody else's son; I wasn't used to it. 'The wheel swings a bit,' I said, 'before it engages.'

'We're so high up,' he said.

'We're kings of the road!'

Ahead of us, fireworks exploded into the sky; stars shot off in all directions.

'It's a bit of a pigsty,' I said. 'I've been driving it for a week.'

'Wish it was light,' he said, 'and my friends could see me.'

I wondered if anyone would ever hear what had happened to me, this past eight days; probably not. I remembered Butler, hiding behind the seats.

'I've met some old mates of yours,' I said. 'Though you'd probably not remember them. Turn left.'

I slowed down, and he turned the wheel. We

262

drove up the adjoining street to Leaps Road, and crawled once more around the block.

'Where did you like living best?' I asked.

He shrugged. We turned left, into his own street. I took the wheel from him and parked the coach.

'Reading, Spalding?' I asked. 'Here?'

'I liked living with Aunty Bun.'

'Hilda?' I switched off the engine. There was silence. He stayed sitting beside me.

'Wish I still lived with Hildy,' he said.

'Why?'

He shrugged, and pulled at a loose thread in his trousers. 'She cooked nice things, and she always had time. She liked watching TV with me.' He wiped his nose. 'She mended my clothes. She knew all the names of my friends. She wasn't on the phone all the time.'

'What about your Mum?'

He pulled a face.

'Well?' I asked.

He sighed, and said: 'She's all right.'

There was a silence. Behind one of the houses there was a red glow; someone had lit a bonfire.

'It's just—' He stopped.

'What?'

'There's never anything in the fridge.' He sniffed. 'And she took away my gun.'

*   *   *

263

Hilda was frying sausages, with Vicky helping.

'This place!' she said. 'There was nothing here. We had to buy these at the corner shop, didn't we, Vicks?'

'Where's Lesley?' I asked.

'She doesn't like the smell,' said Edward. 'She's a vegetarian.'

He started unpacking the box. He laid the fireworks on the table, gloatingly, grading them according to size.

The bottle of port had gone. I looked at Hilda's broad back, as she stood at the oven. The little girl stood beside her, on a chair, a tea-towel wrapped around her waist. She had an implement, too, and pushed the sausages around the pan. She was humming, tunelessly, to herself.

I suddenly felt sad. Here I was—a father, of sorts. A father for tonight, anyway. A bonfire-night father. Here Lesley was, a mother. For better or worse, she had struggled through and had two sturdy children. Whatever their complaints, they would be hers for life. And there stood Hilda, born to be a mother; the most suitable parent of us all.

I thought of Lesley's book, *The Perversity of Desire*, and cursed myself. I cursed the lot of us. Life's unfair, I'd repeated, over and over, these past two months. Of course it bloody was.

There was a hiss, as Hilda turned the sausages. 'This morning, when I was waiting

264

for you,' she said, 'I had a natter with the manager.'

'What?' I asked.

'The hotel manager. They're looking for a new pastry chef. He's giving me a trial run next month.' She inspected the sausages. 'Bugger the Gas Board.'

'You're coming to live in Deal?'

'I've got to get out of my flat anyway,' she said. 'They're pulling it down.' She paused. 'I've missed them.'

I nodded. 'They've missed you.'

She wiped her hands on her apron, and turned to me. 'Lesley's getting on better with her parents,' she said. 'Bodes well for you.'

'Why?'

'Why, nitwit?' She rolled her eyes heavenwards. 'It means she's growing up, doesn't it.'

* * *

Lesley was out in the garden. I saw the red tip of her cigarette.

'He's making garlic bread with Hilda,' I said. I paused, then I sat down beside her on the patio. The concrete was freezing. 'What are we going to tell him?'

'Nothing, yet,' she said.

'What am I going to do?'

'Nothing, yet.'

'I'm selling my house, I'm leaving my job. I

265

can do anything. I can set up a driving school in Deal.' I paused, and added, with the old bitterness: 'I'm fancy free.'

She didn't reply. In the next garden, flames leaped. She passed me the bottle of port and I took a gulp. I felt nervous.

'I hated you for years,' I said.

'No you didn't.'

'I did!'

She sighed. 'You didn't think about me enough to hate me. I bet you didn't.' She ground out her cigarette; sparks flew. 'Not until things went wrong.'

'What do you mean?'

'You know what I mean,' she said.

'I don't.'

She said: 'Until you broke up with your wife.'

I paused. 'What?'

She snorted. 'Men!' she said. 'You're so linear.'

I laughed. 'Never been called that before. What's it in English?'

'Stupid.' She took back the bottle, wiped its lip, with unflattering thoroughness, and drank. 'Dense, Unaware.'

We sat for a moment in silence. Behind us, the light from the kitchen cast our two, humped shadows on to the concrete. Over the fence, sparks flew and children shouted.

'You weren't really looking for your son,' she said.

266

'I was!'

She shook her head.

'What do you mean?' I cried. 'Of course I was!'

She shook her head. 'You were looking for something you'd lost, but it wasn't Edward.'

I paused. 'What was it then?' I asked irritably.

She poked me with her stubby finger. 'Something in there.'

*   *   *

In places, the fence was broken. Through the gaps I could see flames. A rocket zipped up into the sky and there was an *aaah*, like exhaled breath. Like a wave, spilling from the sea and then sighing as it is pulled back again.

For a moment I didn't reply. Then I said, 'Whatever it is, I'm here now.'

We sat there for a while. My body ached. I hadn't had much sleep; on the other hand, I seemed to have slept for months.

Edward was laughing. I could hear him behind me, through the window. All of a sudden my throat swelled up.

Then we heard footsteps and Edward stood in front of us.

'Come on,' he said to me. 'I thought we were making a bonfire.'

He pulled me to my feet; his hand was dry and ruthless.

'Ouch!' I said. I was going to say: my back hurts. But then I thought: bugger my back.

'Come on,' he said, pulling me across the concrete. We stepped onto the soggy lawn.

I gripped his hand; with my other hand I furtively wiped my nose. Thank goodness it was dark and nobody could see. He'd think I was such a sissy.

Sniffing, I walked with him across the grass.

'Afterwards,' he said, 'I'll show you my room.'

CHAPTER TWENTY-FOUR

I gave Edward his first driving lesson today. I must say, he's a better pupil than his mother ever was. We crawled over the sand dunes in one of my Metros; he waved hand signals at the passing gulls. He's got this pink stuff he dabs on his pimples; when we stopped he looked at himself in the driving mirror and asked me if his spots showed. 'No,' I lied.

Should I have told him the truth? Lesley's told him so much. He knows everything about the holes in the ozone layer and the faithlessness of fathers; I feel I must protect him somewhere. His growing-up breaks my heart; he fills me with joy. Perhaps that's because I'm new to it.

Recently, actually, I've begun to get irritated

with him. He watches TV all the time, and when I try to use the stapler there aren't any staples left in it. One of the things I've learnt: a child is different from an adult because nothing stays the way you left it—the toolbox, the dials on your radio. For the first months I was so nice to him that it felt as if we were in some Doris Day film, when it's always a sunny Saturday and nobody can breathe. Sometimes now, when I nag him, I sound just like the parents I used to hear in Croxley Road, when I hadn't a clue about anything. I almost sound like a father.

Hilda and I look after him during the week, while Lesley's in London. He doesn't seem to think this is funny. After all, marriage is a weird enough arrangement—Stan, one of my drivers, he's just got hitched to his divorced wife's sister.

Or, more to the point: every arrangement is a weird sort of marriage. Hilda's and mine is. It seems to be based on loving Ovaltine and Edward. We sleep in twin beds (well, there's no other room in Leaps Road), and at night we read each other bits from our books. I'm sure there's something not very ongoing, as Lesley might say, about all this, but who's she to talk? We gossip about the awful women Lesley brings down from London, where she's running a course on campaigning for crèches (she never made a go of the junk shop). She's taken Vicky with her, but Edward couldn't go because of his school. Anyway, he didn't want to.

Edward is a teenager! I'll practically be a grandfather before I've been a father! It's dusk. We drive back home, past a row of bungalows and some dry trees, bent by the wind. I know every inch of these roads; I've juddered along them a hundred times with my learner drivers.

Edward slots in one of his cassettes. Despite a two-year campaign he still jeers at my taste in music and I jeer at his. In the windows, lights are being switched on.

'*Woo-aaa,*' moans the tape. '*Worjame grinda ja-way gang . . .*'

Sometimes I still believe that, inside those houses, people know the secrets that I've never learnt. In a moment, either a) all will be revealed, or b) it will be too late, and Edward will be a grown man with children of his own and I'll never have caught up.

'*Manarje manarje . . .*' it goes, or something like that.

'You understand this?' I ask.

He shakes his head.

'I used to get the words all wrong. There was this song, "Poetry in Motion"—'

'Dad!' he groans. 'You've told me.'

We pass a lit phone booth; there's a pram parked beside it, and a young woman talking. What happened to that girl in the Bed and Breakfast place? People stay fixed in your

270

mind, frozen at the moment you saw them, but in fact her baby will be a young child by now and she could be anywhere in Britain. Funny, the turnings you take. If I hadn't turned off the M1, that Monday—if I'd driven straight on, back to the depot . . .

The other funny thing: I feel younger, nowadays, than I felt all those years I was married.

We stop outside the house and I switch off the engine. Edward gets out. He's going to be taller than me, and darker; he's already putting that gel stuff on his hair. But, when he smiles, you can see the resemblance.

'My ankles are all achey from the pedals,' he says.

'That's because you've just started. You're just a little squit.' I lock up the car. 'But you'll learn.'